Prewitt shifted beneath the Bookkeeper's suddenly piercing gaze.

"Today you reached the Age of Hope. It's a better day than most for a brave act—or a foolish one."

"How did you know?"

"I'm a collector of stories. What better tale than a Bargeboy and a Princess born under the same moon?"

Prewitt felt a jolt of synchronicity. Granny Arila had said nearly the same thing.

The Bookkeeper stood, and he came so close that Prewitt could feel the heat of his breath on his cheeks. "Tell me, Bargeboy, are you ready to risk everything you know, everything you love, even your own life, for what you seek?"

Prewitt swallowed. "Yes," he said, with more conviction than he felt.

The Bookkeeper grinned, and the effect was ghoulish in the red light.

"Then it's time. Follow me."

—from *The Firebird Song*

BLOOMSBURY PUBLISHING

TITLE: The Firebird Song

AUTHOR: Arnée Flores

ISBN: 978-1-5476-0512-5

FORMAT: hardcover middle grade novel

TRIM: 5 1/2" x 8 1/4"

HC PRICE: $16.99 U.S. / $22.99 CAN.

PUB DATE: May 4, 2021

PAGE COUNT: 288

AGES: 8-11

GRADES: 3-6

CONTACT: ChildrensPublicityUSA@bloomsbury.com

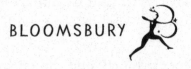

THE FIREBIRD SONG

THE
FIREBIRD
SONG

ARNÉE FLORES

BLOOMSBURY
CHILDREN'S BOOKS
NEW YORK LONDON OXFORD NEW DELHI SYDNEY

BLOOMSBURY CHILDREN'S BOOKS
Bloomsbury Publishing Inc., part of Bloomsbury Publishing Plc
1385 Broadway, New York, NY 10018

BLOOMSBURY, BLOOMSBURY CHILDREN'S BOOKS, and the Diana logo
are trademarks of Bloomsbury Publishing Plc

First published in the United States of America in May 2021
by Bloomsbury Children's Books

Bloomsbury books may be purchased for business or promotional use.
For information on bulk purchases please contact Macmillan Corporate and
Premium Sales Department at specialmarkets@macmillan.com

Library of Congress Cataloging-in-Publication Data
Names: Flores, Arnée, author.
Title: The Firebird song / by Arnée Flores.
Description: New York : Bloomsbury Children's Books, 2021.
Summary: Tied by destiny, Prewitt the Bargeboy and Calliope the Lost Princess set out on their
twelfth birthdays, determined to end the reign of the evil Spectress and her marauders by calling
the Firebird back to Lyrica.
Identifiers: LCCN 2020040637 (print) | LCCN 2020040638 (e-book)
ISBN 978-1-5476-0512-5 (hardcover) • ISBN 978-1-5476-0513-2 (e-book)
Subjects: CYAC: Fantasy.
Classification: LCC PZ7.1.F59427 Fir 2021 (print) | LCC PZ7.1.F59427 (e-book) |
DDC [Fic]—dc23
LC record available at https://lccn.loc.gov/2020040637

Book design by Jeanette Levy
Typeset by Westchester Publishing Services
Printed and bound in the U.S.A. by Berryville Graphics Inc., Berryville, Virginia
2 4 6 8 10 9 7 5 3 1

All papers used by Bloomsbury Publishing Plc are natural, recyclable
products made from wood grown in well-managed forests. The manufacturing
processes conform to the environmental regulations of the country of origin.

To find out more about our authors and books visit
www.bloomsbury.com and sign up for our newsletters.

To Miah, for giving me hope that I could do anything,
and to Heather, for never making me be brave alone

THE FIREBIRD SONG

UNDER THE CALDERA
A LONG TIME AGO

The Demon gnashed its black teeth as it sank beneath the molten surface. It howled, and raged, and fought against the chains that bound it, but it was no use. They had been forged by hope.

What had gone wrong? The Demon still couldn't understand. The darkness had nearly been complete. But this time, at the last moment, just as the Demon was certain it had won, the Firebird had returned to defeat it once again. The unfairness of it all made the Demon weep. Tarry tears splattered and sizzled against its leathery skin.

Since the dawn of time, when the Demon had opened its eyes and felt the realms pulsating with potential for good or evil, the Firebird had been there, too. They were twin creatures born from a single spark of the Great Emperor's campfire: one the embodiment of hope, the other a manifestation of fear.

But while the Firebird flew freely between the realms, singing its interminable Song of Hope, the Demon was forced to wait for an invitation. As the Firebird got fat on the golden apples from the Halcyon Tree that grew at the center of the Emperor's garden, watered by the hope of all realms, the Demon was left to wander, ravenous in the void.

There were no apples for it, no magical songs that caused spring to sprout and spirits to rise from nothing, no magic that allowed the Demon to create at all. Its powers lay in destruction.

It whispered and waited in the void until finally a crack formed, allowing it to slip into a new realm. Humanity had answered its call, and the Demon was finally free to do what it was made to do.

Of course humans had been the key. They always were. They were born fearful, and that fear enabled the Demon to ignite chaos. They ravaged and razed and, in the process, destroyed themselves and the very land that prospered them. It was a feast of power, and the Demon ate its fill. It gorged and gorged until there was no hope left in all the realm.

At last, the Firebird was the one trapped and starving in the void.

Even the Ancient Spirits, the first and most magical of the Firebird's creations, were not able to summon the Firebird. They used every power they knew to entice it to return, but they were not strong enough to overcome the fear and chaos the Demon wrought.

But then somehow, without any warning—out of nowhere!—the Firebird returned.

The Demon still couldn't understand it. All hope had been snuffed out. It should have won! But—

Ah, he remembered now.

A girl. A child so small, the Demon could have stepped on her without noticing. She couldn't have been older than twelve in human years, but she had done the impossible.

She had called the Firebird back.

The Demon shook its head. Enough with these thoughts. What did it matter? This was a dance he knew all too well. He'd memorized every step by rote, and fear could never be kept still for long.

Perhaps the Demon's power could not free it from the Firebird's prison, but it could still be given to the right servant, and then what had been started could begin again.

One child was nothing, meaningless. Soon she would die, and humankind would forget what she had done. Humans never learned, not really.

The Demon chuckled. It howled. It hooted.

Yes, the Demon's time would come again. It had only to whisper, to lift up its voice through the cracks and crevices in the earth, and eventually its call would catch hold. Someone would hear and come to share its power.

Then, at last, the Demon would have its revenge.

1

Lyrica was no place for questions and certainly not one for answers. But Prewitt's curiosity was greater than his fear, and he couldn't stop the words from rushing out with a puff of breath in the dark.

"Granny Arila, won't you tell me what happened that night? The night of the Terrible Thing?" No one had ever told him the story before. He had caught fragments, frightened whispers that trailed off when he came near, but that was all.

A golden Feather, a terrible curse, a Thief who had come in the night.

But no matter how he prodded for details about the Terrible Thing, mouths promptly pressed shut and doors slammed in his face.

For a moment, he wasn't sure the old woman had heard, but finally she nodded. "Yes, you should know. It is time."

Prewitt gulped, biting his tongue to keep from shouting his excitement, afraid that any sound might change Granny Arila's mind.

He moved eagerly forward, clinging to the words that creaked from her cracked lips as she began.

"The Queen should have fled the castle—she might have been safe, but for some reason she chose to stay, as did the King and all their guards and servants. In the end, there was nothing we could do but listen as their screams floated down to our hiding place in the cove.

"We watched the Six Seeking Sailors make their way around the moon, the same path they have always taken on winter's longest night, but just as the sixth star reached its apex, the sky turned to smoke and swallowed the moon. It was darkness like we'd never known. Our lungs filled with ash so thick, we could barely breathe, and we begged the Great Emperor to send his Firebird to save us. But it did not come.

"People whispered that this must be what had been prophesied, the legendary warning of doom that no human ear had ever heard, the one that had sent half the Ancient Spirits fleeing across the sea before the crown of pearls had settled on the first Queen's head."

Thunder boomed, shaking the hut, and Granny Arila continued.

"When, at last, we came out from the cove, the world as we knew it was gone. Everything was gray and bleak, and nature was in chaos. A woman calling herself *the Spectress* perched on the battlements, her face hidden behind a glittering veil. No one knew who she was.

"They only knew that somehow she had awoken the Demon of Fear and used its power to send monstrous ash golems swelling from the castle fireplaces. In the end, the castle was littered with bodies so charred that no one could tell queen from servant or king from guard."

Prewitt's eyes widened.

"Shall I stop?"

He shook his head, afraid to speak lest she change her mind.

"Most troubling of all were the words we found scrawled across the nursery wall in the Queen's own hand: *Wind. Woman. Thief.*"

"What do they mean?" asked Prewitt.

Granny Arila shook her head. "No one knows. They had clearly been written in her last moments, a message, a warning perhaps. But before we could search for more clues, the Spectress's marauders came and forced us from the castle."

Lightning flashed, illuminating the dark room, and the old woman shivered.

"I miss fire. You won't believe me, but fire was once a comfort. It blazed in our homes and down across the beach. We had candles in our windows and fireworks in our skies. Now, look at us, afraid of the feeblest spark."

Her teeth chattered, and Prewitt jumped to his feet. "I'll grab more blankets."

She waved at him. "Nothing can warm these old bones anymore. Sit down. I've more to say and no more time."

Prewitt hesitated. He had been keeping her company for nearly a week, holding her hand and watching her skin grow thin and translucent as she slowly disappeared. He knew she was right. Her time was running short.

Granny Arila peered at him. "Do you know why we're forbidden to speak of the old times? Why the Spectress sent her marauders to burn the books and cast the instruments into the sea? Why minstrels were tossed from the cliffs and singing became a crime punishable by death?"

Prewitt frowned and shook his head.

The old woman pressed a tremulous finger to her heart. "Because she will do anything to keep us hopeless."

"Why?" asked Prewitt.

Granny Arila leaned forward, whispering. "Hope is the thing the Spectress fears most. She knows that hope is the most powerful magic in all of Lyrica, far more powerful than the dark magic she wields—and she will do anything to burn it away. It was hope that called the Firebird back to Lyrica during the last Dark Age, hope held in the heart of a little girl."

Prewitt frowned. He had never heard of the Dark Age before.

Granny Arila nodded. "Times of fear and darkness rise and fall just as the day dawns and sets, and we watch but we do not learn. Humans and spirits take so much for granted, and it is only time and suffering that reminds us. Round and round again."

She broke off, coughing, shuddering wet hacks that shook her frail shoulders. For a moment, it seemed she might wrack herself apart.

But finally, she caught her breath, falling back onto the pillow, thin gray hair sticking to her damp forehead.

"I was once the Singer. Did you know that?"

Prewitt shook his head.

"It was a great honor. It was not an inherited post like you becoming the Bargemaster someday or like the Bookkeeper, whose family has kept the books since the very first Firebird Queen. No, I was *chosen* when I was only five years old. My mother was so proud. I sang for three generations of Queens. I should have been the one to sing the new Princess's name into the world. But I never got the chance."

Granny Arila fell silent, her rheumy eyes awash with memories, and for a moment, he wasn't sure if she was entirely there with him.

She struggled to stand up, and Prewitt rushed to help her as she pressed her bare feet to the rotting slats. She doddered on bony legs, her weight on him. Her breathing was labored, and he saw that she was shaking badly. She was not well.

"I should get my father," he said.

Granny Arila ignored him, teetering toward the back wall of the hut where lichen swelled across molding wood. She pointed an arthritic finger.

Prewitt leaned in, squinting. Thousands of tiny lines were etched like ants across the wood. Granny Arila reached out, scratching one last line into the soft cedar with a blue-tinged fingernail.

"Tomorrow, our Lost Princess reaches the Age of Hope at last."

Goose bumps prickled Prewitt's arms. "But the Princess died on the night of—of the Terrible Thing." He knew that much. It was common knowledge that all the royals had been killed.

"Are you certain?" Granny Arila tilted her head. "Then tell me, why are there no girls your age in the entire kingdom?"

Prewitt frowned. She was right. The only girls he had ever met were either much older or much younger.

Granny Arila reached out and squeezed his hand tight, her eyes boring into him. "The marauders came for the little girls. Parents were so desperate to save them that they abandoned their babies to the woods, praying to anyone and everyone— even the Wild Woman herself—for help. Those who were brave enough to keep their children at their breasts paid with their lives, and their precious girls were taken."

Prewitt's eyes widened. "Why?"

"Why do you think?"

An invisible breeze swept through the hut, rustling the damp curtains, and the hairs on Prewitt's arms lifted.

"The Spectress is searching for the Lost Princess?"

"Yes," said the old woman.

"She survived!" Prewitt couldn't believe it. How was it possible? How could a baby live through something so horrible?

Granny Arila's grip tightened on his hand. "But the Spectress has run out of time. Legend says that when a daughter of a Firebird Queen reaches the Age of Hope, she comes into her powers and is able to call the Firebird back."

Prewitt looked at the lines etched in the wall, trying to make sense of everything Granny Arila had told him. "I'll be twelve tomorrow, too," he said. "I wonder why no one ever told me we were born on the same day."

Granny Arila's eyes sparkled. "You're the Bargeboy and a special one at that. Destiny has big plans for you."

Prewitt laughed. He couldn't help it. He wasn't special. He might be the Bargeboy, but he'd never even seen the *Queen's Barge*. He'd never been anywhere.

Granny Arila shook her head. "You mustn't laugh. The Princess and her Bargeboy have always been tied. Somewhere, even now, she may be waiting for you."

Prewitt looked back at the lines on the wall. Was it possible? "My dad doesn't believe in destiny," he said. "He told me duty is what matters. It's what keeps us from going down the wrong path."

Granny Arila's eyes lifted to the window. "Look up there," she said. "What do you see?"

Prewitt shook his head. "Nothing. There's nothing there. Just clouds like always."

Granny Arila shook her head. "You can't see it, but I can."

She closed her eyes. "Yes, there she is." Her mouth spread into a smile. "The moon's face always shone through that window." Granny Arila opened her eyes and looked at Prewitt. "I can still see her despite the clouds, just as I see you, Bargeboy."

"What? What do you see?" he asked. She wasn't making any sense.

"I see your destiny. I see who you can become. *The moon's halves must be united.* That's what the prophecy foretold. You and the Princess."

Granny Arila's coughing began again, shaking her entire body. She leaned against the wall to keep from falling and slid into a damp heap on the floor.

"Granny Arila?" Prewitt asked, still holding her frail hand. It was ice-cold. He crouched beside her. "Please let me go and get my father now."

Granny Arila nodded, giving him a weak smile. "Go on, then, Bargeboy." She leaned back against the wall and closed her eyes.

Prewitt ran out across the Royal City tier. The hazy night glowed red in the flickering light from the city lantern, and the puddles glinted like spinning Catherine wheels as the rain *shush*ed and his boots smacked along the tier.

The Cursed Castle loomed menacing and black-faced at the top of the cliff.

Prewitt knew death. All Lyrican children recognized it as it came sweeping through the night, curving through the streets,

11

twisting an indiscriminate path down from the ever-turbulent sky, unstoppable as the rain.

The sea groaned and the wind keened as he burst through the door into his rickety house.

"Emperor above, Prewitt!" scolded his mother. "Hush before you wake your sister."

"Where's Dad?" gasped Prewitt. "The Singer is dying!"

The mending slipped from his mother's fingers. "Where did you hear that name?" she whispered, casting a terrified glance at the door. "You mustn't call her that."

"I *need* Dad!" Prewitt repeated.

"Your father's still out."

Prewitt hopped from foot to foot. "But he *has* to come!"

Prewitt's mother stood and walked a few steps, grabbing a heap of worn blankets from the mattress on the floor. "Calm down. It's going to be all right," she soothed, piling the blankets into his arms. "All you can do is make her as warm as you can and keep her company. She has no one else. People are too afraid of the Spectress's rules, of the consequences. But you are small. You can slip in and out without being seen. She knows you. She trusts you."

"But—"

"Be brave, Prewitt. There's nothing to be afraid of. This is the normal way of life. I promise I'll send your father as soon as he returns."

Prewitt ran back outside, not bothering to shut the door behind him. The spirit chimes jangled in the doorframe, calling out to others across the tiers.

He turned back toward Granny Arila's hut, but his feet slowed. A strange sound weaved its way through the rain. It was a voice, but the sound it made was like nothing Prewitt had ever heard.

Rise up, my budding Lyrica
Rise up to meet the sea
Sing not a song of mourning
She'll soon return to thee

Someone was *singing*, Prewitt suddenly realized. *Singing* even though it was forbidden. He had never heard any music before, not even the simplest child's song, and he stood transfixed in the downpour. The ocean spat foam on the tiers, and crows shrieked from the trees at the top of the cliff.

Rise up, my budding Lyrica
Rise up to meet the tide
For nigh the Barge is coming
And upon it she will ride

The melody cut through the storm, strong and defiant, and the hairs on Prewitt's arms lifted.

Faces appeared in windows, fear-white and gaping, and all around, shutters slammed shut against Granny Arila's song.

"Prewitt!"

His mother grasped his wrist. She had been calling his name, but he had not heard.

"You have to stop her!" she said. "Go! Run! Quickly, before the marauders hear!"

Prewitt dropped the blankets and bolted.

The Singer's voice was full and broad, and the vibrato rumbled through Prewitt's heart like thunder as his boots threw up mud.

He skidded to a stop in front of Granny Arila's hut just as she stumbled into the doorway, leaning heavily against the rotting doorframe. A piece of the lintel splattered into the muck, but she did not stop singing.

He grabbed her arm. "Please, Granny Arila, you have to stop! Come back inside!"

But it was too late. Heavy metal boots sloshed and slapped down the city steps from the Cursed Castle. A sudden sheet of lightning lit slate-spiked armor, and steel gloves flashed as the Spectress's marauders marched nearer.

Prewitt cringed back against the hut, but Granny Arila did not shrink away. She gazed across at him. "Go home, Bargeboy."

Prewitt shook his head. "Please don't do this."

Granny Arila pressed her lips together. "I am the Singer. I will not die silenced in the damp."

She reached out and brushed his cheek with her finger. It came back wet and shining, and she pressed it to her lips. "Remember, Bargeboy. The greatest duty of all is to accept your destiny. You *must* find the Princess."

Prewitt sobbed, desperate. The marauders had nearly reached them. He tried again to pull Granny Arila inside. "Please, please—"

She gave him a little push, water sloshing up as he splashed down into the mud.

"Go. Go and *remember*."

She turned away from him, toward the approaching marauders, her face peaceful and unafraid.

In her fist will be the Feather
In her heart will be the Song
And the Spirits will rejoice
And all hope shall be made strong

Prewitt fought with himself. He could stay, he could fight, but what good would it do? He was just one boy, and he wasn't very big or strong. He couldn't fight the Spectress's men all alone. He didn't even know how to fight. In the end, he fled. He ran as fast as he could away from the clattering armor and down the abandoned street.

He wanted to scream at all the people who had closed themselves behind shuttered windows, to force them to come out and do something. What could he do on his own?

He tripped over his feet and fell to his knees in the muck.

A strong hand grabbed his arm and yanked him to his feet.

Prewitt's father frowned down at him. "Prewitt! Thank the Emperor." His mustache and cap poured rain, and his face was grave.

"Dad!" said Prewitt, weak with relief. "You have to help her!"

"There is nothing I can do." He pulled Prewitt across the tier.

"But you're the Bargemaster. They'll listen to you!"

His father shook his head. "That doesn't mean anything to them, Prewitt."

Prewitt tried to jerk away, tried to run back to Granny Arila, but his father lifted him off his feet and slung him over his back.

His father sprinted to the house, flinging Prewitt down, and spun to bar the door. Prewitt's mother had already closed the shutters, and now the house was nothing but shapes and shadows.

Prewitt pushed himself to his feet and scrambled up the loft ladder.

"Prewitt, don't!" shouted his father.

Prewitt ignored him. He crawled past his sleeping sister and across the boards to the octagon window. A tin bucket pinged as rain bled through the rotting rafters.

He could just make out the marauders through the haze. They stood in a semicircle around Granny Arila's hut.

Her song did not falter as they took their positions.

It will return on wings of flame
And our tears will be no more

They raised metal fists in the air.

When at last our Queen comes home

16

Steel gloves struck down across flint spikes.

And the Firebird rides to shore.

Sparks erupted in a bright shower. They hung, bulging and swelling, twisting into enormous, smoky shapes that Prewitt couldn't fully make out through the mist. He pressed his nose to the glass. From afar, he saw flickering veins of fire coursing through hulking giants of smoke and ash.

Prewitt knew at once that these were the Spectress's ash golems. He held his breath as the monsters turned to face Granny Arila. They opened yawning mouths, and Prewitt saw that their bellies were full of boiling lava.

All at once, they attacked, spewing flame.

Prewitt cried out, but before he could see what happened, he was yanked roughly away from the window. His father's calloused hand pressed hard against his eyes.

Prewitt tried to pull away, but his father held him tight.

"Don't look. This is nothing a child should see."

There was a horrible, echoing scream, and then Prewitt could hear nothing but the pinging of the bucket and the sea's steady groan beneath the clanging spirit chimes.

2

"How could you let them do that?" Prewitt seethed after his father had released him and the marauders returned to their posts. "You could have stopped them!"

The Bargemaster's eyes shifted to Pyper, somehow still fast asleep on her bedraggled mattress. "Let's talk about this below, Prewitt."

Prewitt opened his mouth to argue, but his mother called his name from the kitchen—just once, soft and urgent—and Prewitt pressed his lips tight as he climbed reluctantly back down from the loft.

But the moment his feet pressed to the slats, the words burst out. *"You should have done something!"*

His father's boots *thunk*ed to the floor as if their weight was too much for his legs. He sighed, turning to Prewitt. "Granny Arila knew what she was doing. She knew what would happen if she sang that song, but she chose to leave the world on her own terms, to—"

"I needed you! I came looking for you, and you were gone!"

"You know I can't always be here, Prewitt."

His mother nodded. "Lots of people need your father, Witty. They need someone to turn to, and he's all they have left. We mustn't be selfish—"

"But I'm your son! Doesn't that mean anything at all?"

His father's eyes were sad. "Of course it does, Prewitt."

"You should have been here."

"There wasn't anything I could have done."

Prewitt folded his arms, swallowing the lump in his throat. Was that it, then? They would all just sit back while the Spectress's marauders bullied them, and hurt them, and *killed* them? While the weather got worse? While the food ran out? Was there truly nothing they could do?

The greatest duty of all is to your destiny. Prewitt leaned forward on his toes. "We could find the Lost Princess," he whispered. "She reaches the Age of Hope tomorrow just like me! She'll be able to call the Firebird back!"

Prewitt's mother gasped and covered her mouth, and the Bargemaster's face turned to stone. "Prewitt," he said, his tone overly patient. "You know the Princess died during the Terrible—"

"No!" Prewitt leaned in, needing his father to understand. "Granny Arila told me she survived! Don't you see? That's why the Spectress took all the little girls. She was looking for *her*!"

Prewitt squinted to see his father's reaction in the dark, but what he found unnerved him. "You already knew," he accused.

The Bargemaster cleared his throat, and when he spoke, his voice was rough. "Granny Arila should never have told you that. She shouldn't have gotten your hopes—"

"Why not?" demanded Prewitt. "Granny Arila said it's my destiny to find her! She said we're two halves of one moon."

"No, Prewitt. Granny Arila may have believed in destiny, but I do not. It is our duty to—"

"Duty! That's all you ever talk about. Wasn't it your duty as the Bargemaster to keep the Princess safe in the first place? You have to at least try to find her! If she really is out there somewhere, then the Spectress—"

The Bargemaster's jaw clenched. "I know you're upset, son, but you aren't thinking clearly. If the Spectress hasn't found the Princess by now, how will you? Besides, even if we wanted to, even if we knew where to begin searching, we couldn't. We're cut off from the other cities. The forest is overgrown, and the sailors can barely survive the sea long enough to catch fish to feed us all."

"We could go upriver!" said Prewitt. "We could take the *Queen's Barge*! She's the best boat in the kingdom!"

His parents were silent in the dark.

Finally his father said, "We can't take the Barge, Prewitt."

"What do you mean? You're the Bargemaster. You can—"

"The marauders are *always* watching. It would be impossible to get to the tunnels and down to the Sacred Cavern without being seen. Besides, I will not risk your life by taking you on a doomed journey up the river. The current is too strong, even for the *Queen's Barge*. It's too dangerous."

Prewitt banged his fist on the table. "Everything is dangerous!"

"Prewitt!" His mother was suddenly beside him, gripping his shoulder hard, her face ghost white. "Spirits guard your tongue! You saw what happened to Granny Arila. They'll do it to you, too. They don't care if you're only a child."

"I'm not afraid," said Prewitt, "and I'm not a child!"

"Listen to me," whispered the Bargemaster. "Maybe you don't care about your own safety, but I know you care about the Barge. If we took her out, the Spectress would destroy her. It's your duty as the Bargeboy to help keep the Barge safe."

"I wouldn't let anything happen." Prewitt tried to keep the whine from his voice. "Don't you trust me?"

His father sighed. "It's not about trust, Prewitt."

"But I should be starting my apprenticeship tomorrow! I'll be twelve. You should be taking me to the Barge anyway!"

"If things were normal, I would be. But they aren't. The fact that you don't seem to grasp the danger of what you're suggesting, even after everything you've just seen, tells me that you're not ready. Reaching the Age of Hope doesn't make you grown up, and it doesn't keep you safe."

"I'm not afraid!"

"You should be afraid!"

"Well, I'm not." The emotions spewed from Prewitt's lips

without thought. "I'm angry! I'm angry that you weren't here when I needed you. I'm angry that you didn't fight for Granny Arila! I'm angry that you won't do anything now! You know what I think? I think *you're* the one who's scared."

The Bargemaster sprang up, knocking over his chair. "Of course I'm scared! My fear keeps us all safe! You don't know what I've given, what I've sacrificed to keep everyone safe."

In the loft, Pyper began to cry, and Prewitt's mother climbed up the ladder to soothe her.

Prewitt's chest felt tight, and his nails dug into his palms.

The Bargemaster's voice was strained. "If you aren't afraid of the Spectress, remember the Demon. It made her what she is. It would do worse than kill you. It would *turn* you. You would forget who you are. You would forget your mother's face and your sister's name. You would know nothing but fear and hatred."

Prewitt scowled. "The Demon couldn't turn me. I wouldn't let it."

"Yes it would." Prewitt's mother leaned over the loft rail with Pyper in her arms. "It would turn you, just like it turned the marauders. They were once fathers who loved their children. Husbands who cared for their wives. They dared to enter the caldera, and now look at them."

Prewitt swallowed. The marauders stalked the city with black eyes and vacant expressions. They never seemed quite human.

The Bargemaster picked up his cap off the table, his

shoulders slumped. "Now, I have to go see what remains of Granny Arila and make preparations to send her bottle to the sea." He moved toward the door, steps heavy. He slid the bolt back, and it banged open in a flurry of wind. The spirit chimes clattered, and he raised his voice against the gale.

"Prewitt, I want you to give me the Waterman's Word that you will not go looking for the *Queen's Barge*. You must forget what you heard about the Lost Princess."

Prewitt didn't answer. The wind screamed like a banshee beyond the door, and Prewitt's throat tightened. "Don't you believe in me at all?" he choked. "I could do it. I know I could. I could find her. Please—"

His father's mouth was a tight line. "Swear, or I will lock you in this house until you do."

"I swear," said Prewitt, holding three fingers to his lips and fighting to keep the tears from spilling onto his cheeks.

"Good." His father sighed. "I know you're angry. I know you don't understand, but I hope someday you will."

With that, the Bargemaster trudged out into the rain, leaving Prewitt alone in the doorway.

3

Prewitt had only ever seen one book.

He didn't know where it had come from. Maybe it had always been there, hiding beneath the musty kitchen floorboards.

When he was very small, he had lain on his stomach for hours, tracing the beautiful illustrations with tiny fingers while his mother scrubbed and scrubbed, trying without success to keep black mold from overtaking the house.

The book was filled with intricate maps of Lyrica. One page showed the three seas, the strange Nymph Isles floating like crescent moons in an ocean sky. Another gave shape to the Two Woods, where keen eyes could spot mysterious creatures bending bright green treetops. There was even one that traced the river, through the steep gorge and between the woods, following the path the Queen had once taken with her watermen on the annual Spring Journey past the seven river cities to the mountains.

But all of these paled in comparison to Prewitt's favorite page: a vibrant, full-color map of the Royal City. One thin piece of parchment lay over another. On the top page, the castle perched merrily atop rows of terraces, smiling down at the sparkling sea where merchant ships lined the harbor and sailors unloaded crates heaped with fabrics, gems, and sweets for the market.

The Firebird Tale and Tome Bookshop stretched up from the beach, story after wonky story, and at the very top, glowing within a brilliant sea-glass dome, was the gleaming city lantern. Prewitt imagined it shining off the page, lighting up their gloomy house.

He had been surprised to see rows of rainbow houses traipsing across the paper on the tiers nearest the castle. When he asked his mother about them, she told him that before the marauders had burned everything to make way for their black-flapped tents, they had lived in the rainbow houses. "It was so wonderful," she said. "Sometimes I think it's a mercy that you don't remember how it was before they burned it all."

The map of the Royal City never quite felt real. The castle he knew was a hulking black tomb, and their homes were cold and colorless and somehow always let the sea in no matter how they fought to keep it out. As hard as he tried, he just couldn't match the images on the page with the drenched and unfriendly place he knew.

But despite how impossible the painted city seemed, Prewitt loved it. Most of all, he loved what lay beneath the top page, for when he pulled the parchment back, a secret world was revealed. Tunnels wound down the page like serpents, twisting in knots and bunches beneath the tiers, and at the very bottom, hidden behind a golden door that could be folded open, was the Sacred Cavern, the *Queen's Barge* floating at its heart like a jewel.

Gold leaf was affixed to the hull with great care, and it didn't take much imagination for Prewitt to feel as if he were seeing the real boat. There was even a tiny Bargemaster standing on the quarterdeck in his red coat, ten blue-clad watermen waiting at the oars for his command.

Prewitt had spent entire days imagining what it would be like to reach the Age of Hope and finally become his father's apprentice. But when the scarce light filtering through the mold-splotched windows faded, the book and his dreams would have to be put back in their place beneath the boards.

One day, when Prewitt was four or five, there had been a pounding on the door, and a distraught man had burst through in a drenched panic.

The man was bent nearly double, and his spotted head shone with rain. A white beard hung down to his knees, and he had to strain to look up at Prewitt's mother through misted oval glasses. "They know!"

Prewitt's mother had ordered him up to the loft in a tone he had never heard her use before, and even though he had tried to hear more of what they were saying, he couldn't make out their voices above the rain hammering the roof.

All he could do was watch as his mother lifted the boards and took out his precious book. She handed it to the old man, who tucked it inside his robe and disappeared into the deluge.

Prewitt demanded to know why his mother had given the man his book, but all she said was, "Thomas will keep it safe. I promise. It's for the best." Prewitt hadn't believed her.

Later, when his father had come in, his face had been drawn. "There was nothing we could do. They found the books in Elinor and Jonah's mattress. We only just saved the boy, Jack. He's with Old Harry now."

His mother wept. "That poor little boy. He's all alone. How will we ever survive this? It will never end. The Spectress will never stop torturing us.

Prewitt had never heard his mother speak that way before, had never seen her cry before, and he cried, too, but his tears were for his beautiful book with the golden door that opened onto the *Queen's Barge*.

He pleaded and pried until, finally, he found out who the old man was: the Bookkeeper. But no one had seen the Bookkeeper outside of his shop since the night he'd come and taken away the forbidden books, and no matter how Prewitt pestered, his mother refused to take him anywhere near the Firebird Tale and Tome. Sometimes Prewitt thought he saw an old man peeking through the shuttered windows, but he could never be sure.

The loft ladder creaked, and Prewitt snapped back to the present as his mother knelt by his mattress. He avoided her eyes as she brushed his hair back with cool, calloused fingers.

"I know it's hard, Witty," she whispered, her breath a white billow in the dark. "I've known Granny Arila my entire life. I—I mean—" She broke off, and her hand fell from Prewitt's forehead. "I *knew* her. She used to bring me yellow daisies. She said that it was her songs that made them that color. I never knew if she was teasing me." She laughed, but her laugh broke off into a sob.

Prewitt's gaze dropped from the rafters. His mother's palms were pressed against her eyes, and they didn't move as she went on, her voice quavering. "It all feels so hopeless. I don't even know who I am anymore. It's as if I've been erased by so many years of fear. Survival has taken all I have, and there isn't anything of *me* left."

She wiped her hands on her tattered skirt and, catching Prewitt's worried gaze, she shook her head and forced a smile to her lips. "I'm sorry. I shouldn't have said any of that."

She leaned down and kissed his forehead. "It's okay. Everything is going to be okay. Now, get some rest. Tomorrow's a big day for you. The Age of Hope. I still can't believe it!" Her voice was cheery but hollow.

Prewitt lay awake long after she had gone, his hands clutching the damp blankets. Somehow, the hopelessness in his mother's voice had pierced him deeper than anything else that had happened.

It was said that there could be no honor in a waterman who broke an oath, but lying on his musty mattress, shivering in the dark, Prewitt wondered if things like honor even mattered anymore. Who cared about oaths in a world where old women were burned to death in the streets? Who cared about duty when mothers hid tears behind their palms and pasted smiles across their sorrow? Did anything even matter in a world where children were kept in the dark with nothing to fill their days but fear and chaos?

His father talked about duty, but what had he done to fulfill his duty as the Bargemaster? He hadn't kept the Princess or the Queen safe. He hadn't kept the city safe.

Prewitt glared at the ceiling. His father might not believe in destiny, but he did. After all, what else was there to believe in? When Granny Arila had looked at him, she had seen something that no one else could, and he was determined to find out what it was.

He didn't need his father's permission to take the Barge. All he needed was a map, and he knew exactly where to find one.

4

The moment Prewitt heard his father's boots *thud* across the wooden floor and caught the telltale click of the front door latch, he flung off his covers and leaped out of bed.

He slipped into his clothes and crept toward the ladder. But before he could climb down, Pyper sat up, her hair rumpled and a huge smile on her face.

"Happy birthday, Pew-it!" she squealed. She launched herself at him, wrapping tiny arms around his legs. Even though she had just climbed out of bed, her hair and nightgown were damp, and Prewitt rubbed at the goose bumps lining her tiny arms, trying to warm her as he shushed. But the more he shushed, the louder she squealed, and soon, Prewitt's mother was awake, too, and insisting he eat breakfast.

"I'm not hungry," Prewitt argued, glancing toward the door. He wanted to get down to the beach before the tide came in and the Bookshop door was blocked. The tides had gotten so high and treacherous that they covered the first three floors of the Firebird Tale and Tome and drenched the houses on the bottom tier.

"Eat anyway," ordered his mother, pulling a fish head from the salt brine and slopping it into a bowl of cold seaweed broth.

There was never any cooked food, no hot soup or rolls fresh from the oven. It wasn't worth the risk of raising the Spectress's golems.

"Don't you want to wait for your father to get home before you run off? I'm sure he'll want to wish you a happy birthday."

"I'm going to help Jack mend the nets," Prewitt said, shoving a large wad of seaweed into his mouth. It squished between his teeth.

"I guess that's all right. That poor boy. He works so hard all the time. Just promise you won't go above the domestic tiers. I don't want you anywhere near the marauders' tents today."

"I promise," said Prewitt.

She watched him for a moment. "Witty," she said slowly. "About last night, I—"

"We don't have to talk about it. It's okay."

His mother looked like she was going to say something more, but instead, she walked over to the little desk nestled in the corner beside his parents' defeated mattress and drew out the drawer. Prewitt watched as she reached into the space where the drawer had been, rapping her knuckles on a wood panel at the back. A hidden compartment popped open, and she pulled out a package.

Prewitt nearly dropped his spoon. He would never have known there was a compartment there.

His mother set the package on the table and kissed the top of his head. "You only reach the Age of Hope once. I thought your father would be back in time to see you open it, but I'm sure he'd like you to have it if you insist on going out right away."

Prewitt tensed as he untied the twine, pulling back the stained silk wrapping. For a moment, he was caught by the thrill of what lay inside. There, neatly folded and bright as the day it was made, was a Bargemaster's coat all in red, the color of yew berries.

He ran his fingers along the mother-of-pearl buttons marching down the breast and along the cuffs. Each one was stamped with an eight-pointed golden star. On the back, the Queen's crest shone in gold thread: two delicate feathers, attached by their quills, framed a long-rooted apple tree, an ornate crown floating above.

A lump rose in Prewitt's throat, and he shoved it away. "What's the point? You heard what Dad said. I'm not starting my apprenticeship. He won't even take me to the Barge."

"Oh, Prewitt. I know it isn't what you hoped for, but it's still something, isn't it? Won't you at least try it on?"

"Please, Pew-it!" begged Pyper.

Prewitt sighed, standing up and slipping his arms into the sleeves.

His mother turned him around to face the mirror, wiping the haze away with her palm.

His heart squeezed, and for a moment, he was speechless.

"There, you see? You look just like your father."

Prewitt caught her eyes in the mirror.

"Please, Prewitt. Won't you at least *try* to be happy? Just for today?" She turned, scrubbing at a spot on the counter.

Prewitt didn't answer. Instead, he slipped out the door and into the rain before he could lose his nerve.

He felt guilty leaving her—lying to her—but it was for a good reason. She would see that soon. Once he found the Princess, they wouldn't have to pretend. His mother's smile would be real.

Prewitt was shocked when not even a single drop of rain found its way through the fabric of his new jacket. For the first time, he was really and truly dry. He pulled it tight as he walked against the wind and shoved his hands into the deep pockets.

The early-morning sky was a dim, drizzling sheet of pre-dawn gray, the color it would remain until the black of night overtook it. Prewitt's mother said that the city lantern had once burned so brightly that it could be seen by sailors ten miles from shore. Now it barely lit the harbor.

Fog bells beckoned one another through the murk as the night boats limped back to harbor and others prepared to take their place. The sea had developed a voracious appetite for boats, devouring them in hungry swells and vomiting rotting fish onto the wet sand. A putrid stench wafted across the tiers.

Few people were out in the early hours. A woman beat wet clothes against the side of her house—*fwap, fwap, fwap*—and pretended not to see him as he passed. A man stumbled from the Drink's Bottom Tavern, vomiting into the mud. Prewitt sidestepped the mess. The man's eyes rolled to meet his, and then he turned and went back inside.

The Royal City residents had once prided themselves on their friendly hospitality, but fear had made them suspicious and surly. Hunger made them miserly, and cold made them bitter. They kept their shawls closed and their children indoors.

Now that he thought about it, Granny Arila was one of only a handful of people who had ever even spoken to him.

He slowed, then stopped, finding himself in front of the Singer's hut—at least, what remained of it. Charred wood settled into the muck, and where Prewitt had last seen the old woman standing, there was only an oozing hole, sloshing with rainwater.

He shivered. Had his father come and taken Granny Arila's body away? Or was this all that remained?

She used to bring me yellow daisies. That's what his mother had said, but Prewitt didn't even know what a daisy looked like.

As he gazed down at the muddy hole, he felt something new slurry in his heart—a secret truth that had been lurking behind blame and anger.

He could have stopped this.

Granny Arila had sent him away, but he could have refused. He could have stayed. He could have at least *tried*.

But he had been afraid, so he had left it to grown-ups to act, and because of that, this puddle was all that remained of the old woman who had been his only friend.

He looked down at his face, warped and splattering in the puddle. What had Granny Arila seen in him? He couldn't see anything at all, just a small, frightened boy with too many freckles.

A metal *clank*ing startled Prewitt from his thoughts, and he turned, his heart beating fast, fists at the ready. He knew that sound. It was the sound that had come before the flames—before the screams—the sound of a marauder's armor.

He squinted, trying to see through the gloom.

"The girl reaches the Age of Hope today. You know what that means."

The voice was coming from the alley a few feet away. Prewitt tried to back up, but his boots squished in the mud. He crouched down, holding his breath.

"Of course I know what it means. The Firebird can return." Bells jangled, a bird screeched, and Prewitt's spine froze. He knew at once who was hiding in the mist with the metal-booted marauder: *The Falconer.*

It wasn't just children who were afraid of the Falconer. His name was Smith, and he was a hulking man with dark eyebrows that grew like thorn bushes above his mean black eyes. Not long after the Terrible Thing, Smith had locked himself inside the falconry at the edge of the abandoned agriculture tier. The chicken houses decayed, the pig huts fell to ruins, and the milking barn blew clean into the sea, but Smith and his falconry endured.

The falcons themselves were legendary. They could deliver messages across the entire kingdom of Lyrica—from sea to mountains—in hours. At least, they could before, but the Terrible Thing had changed everything.

Now, the Falconer refused to send his birds into the weather, no matter how desperate people were to know if their family members in other areas of the kingdom were still alive. They called him cruel, selfish, unfeeling, but the insults slid from his brows like rain as the door slammed in their faces.

On the rare occasion that Smith bothered to descend into the city, he kept to the shadows, dodging rumors that he had begun teaching his birds deadly tricks in his solitude.

The marauder continued, nasally words deliberate. "The girl does not have what she needs to call the Firebird. We still have time."

"What does any of this have to do with me?" growled Smith.

"The Spectress would like me to convey how very grateful she would be for any assistance you might lend in locating the girl," the marauder wheedled. *Very grateful indeed.*"

Smith scoffed. "I'm the last one who would ever help her."

"Oh, I think you might change your mind. You see, she has something you misplaced. Something you had thought *lost for good.*"

There was a sudden, sharp whistle, the screech of a bird, the frantic flapping of wings.

The marauder cried out. "Get it off me, Smith!"

"Why *now*? I've been searching for nearly twelve years!"

There was a choking sound. "It's the truth! I swear it! I've seen with my own eyes. Pahleeease!"

The Falconer whistled once more and the marauder panted. After he had caught his breath, he said, "I could have you burned for that! It's *treason* for your birds to attack me! *Treason!* I'm one of the Spectress's chosen!"

The Falconer was unfazed by the other man's threats. "All this time, I thought . . . Is it possible?" He broke off. "Come. Wherever the Princess is, if she truly is alive, my birds will find her."

The men's voices trailed away, and Prewitt stood, his heart hammering in his chest. What could the Spectress have that the Falconer wanted? Whatever it was, it had been enough for him to betray them all.

A new urgency filled him as he blinked down at the sloshing hole. Granny Arila had believed in him last night and he had failed her, but he wouldn't let her down now. He pressed the backs of three fingers to his lips.

I'm sorry I didn't save you, Granny Arila. But I'm going to find a way to set things right—I swear.

And this time, it was a promise he meant to keep.

5

The Lost Princess did not know she was lost; in fact, she did not know she was a princess at all.

She knew all sorts of other things, like how to climb a steep wall and how to hold her breath underwater for a very long time. She had read many books and lived a thousand different adventures, but she had never gone outside her home.

Only one person ever came to visit. His name was Meredith. Twice a day, when the last grain of sand filtered through her hourglass, he would come, pulling his own identical glass from his pocket. When he left, he would tip Calliope's hourglass over, and she would watch as the sand in his swept back to the top all on its own, a mirror image of hers.

Once, when she was very small, Calliope had grown tired of waiting for Meredith. She had knocked her hourglass on its side, enjoying the way the sand pooled against the crystal.

She'd been thrilled when Meredith had come running through the doors just a few minutes later, out of breath and panicked.

"You must never, *ever* do that again," he had scolded, and by his tone, she knew that she had done something very wrong.

"Please, Mer," she begged over and over. "Why can't I go outside? I don't want to stay here all alone."

But he always said the same thing. "Because you're still just a girl, and I promised your mother I would keep you safe."

He told her that her parents had given their lives to protect her. He said that the world beyond her door was more terrible than anything she could imagine. "There are monsters that would burn you alive in an instant."

Calliope yearned to know more. But her questions had only seemed to make him sad, and she had finally stopped asking.

Instead, she watched and tried to learn what she could on her own.

He was always wet, his clothes soaked through, so Calliope knew that it must rain a lot outside. She tried to imagine rain, but it was impossible to really picture it, the way it fell from the sky. She had never even seen the sky. When she looked up, there was only solid rock.

Meredith's fingers were always cracked and covered in blisters, and his forearms were often bruised. Calliope wondered why. Did he have to fight the monsters? Was that why he walked with heavy feet and held his head as if a great weight rested on it?

Whenever he appeared, his satchel was full of food and books. Calliope adored books. She had stacks and stacks of them. In a way, books were her truest friends—besides her paper animals, of course.

Calliope could make anything from paper. She had made Brown Bear first, and when she showed him to Meredith, he had told her how clever she was. It had taken her days to get the cuts and folds just right, but in the end, she marveled at how lifelike the bear looked with his little glasses and tailored vest. Then she'd made Lion with his shaggy mane and sage advice, and Hippo, who was always good for a laugh. She made all sorts of others, too, a whole menagerie, but the first three were her favorites. They understood her best, maybe because they'd been by her side for such a long time.

At first, it hadn't seemed to bother Meredith that she talked to her animals. But as time went by and Calliope got older, his face grew grim whenever she mentioned them.

Now, the animals were all arranged so that they could be part of a celebration. Today was a big day.

"I'm finally twelve years old," she told them. "All the books say that's the time when extraordinary things happen. They call it the *Age of Hope*."

She leaned toward them. "Today, I'm going to ask Meredith to take me with him when he leaves." She had been thinking about it for a long time, daydreaming about the moment when she could finally step out into the world beyond the door. "He won't say no," she said. "Not today."

The final grain of sand slipped down to join the heap at the bottom of the glass, and Calliope went to wait by the door. Soon, the gentle tap came, and she opened it, letting Meredith squeeze through.

"Mer!" she cried, flinging herself into his arms.

After he had removed his boots, and once they were seated at the table, Meredith pulled a salt-crusted fish from his satchel, and Calliope bounced in her chair. "You haven't forgotten what day it is today, have you?"

Meredith reached up to rub his forehead, and she saw that his blistered hands were covered in black dirt. Calliope watched as his jaw clenched, and she noticed that the circles under his eyes were darker than usual, his face creased more deeply.

She jumped up and ran around the table, draping her arms across his shoulders. "What's wrong?"

He reached up and patted her hand. "Nothing is wrong," he said. "Sit back down. There's something I have to tell you."

Calliope sat, tugging one of her curls.

Meredith kneaded his temples, trying to think of what to say. All these years, he'd been plagued by the guilt of leaving her behind. It followed him into the world, dogging his steps with doubt and uncertainty. But no matter how tempted he was to bring her out into the light, he couldn't abandon his duty. What if something happened to her? How could he live with himself?

Calliope's stomach twisted. "Mer? What's going on?"

He cleared his throat. "Calliope, today you're the Age of

Hope, and I must tell you something, something I should have told you a long time ago."

"What is it?" asked Calliope. She suddenly had the feeling that he was going to tell her something terrible.

He paused, opening and closing his mouth as if he were trying to speak, but the words wouldn't come.

"You don't have to tell me," she said, patting his hand. "It's okay."

"No, I do. Do you still have the book? The one I told you to keep safe?"

"Of course," said Calliope. She remembered the day he'd given it to her. It hadn't been long after she'd tipped over the hourglass and brought him running through the doors. It was the first book he had ever brought in his satchel.

She hadn't even known how to read yet, but she had understood that the book was very important because Meredith's face had been so serious. "You must put this book someplace safe and only read it if a day and a night pass and I do not come—do you understand?"

Calliope had been confused. Why wouldn't he come? He always came. But she had done as he asked. When she had finally learned to read, she had pulled out the book. She had felt guilty doing it, but her guilt soon turned to disappointment when she saw that the book wasn't anything extraordinary. It wasn't that different from all her other books, just superstitions and tales. Like all the others, it spoke of things she had never seen or felt like the sea, the wind, and the rain. Things she could experience only in her mind.

She went to get it now, setting it in front of Meredith on the table.

There was something in the way his hand shook, in the way he looked at the book like its pages held the greatest tragedy, that made her want to take it and put it back in its place.

After a long moment, he opened it to the very back, running a dirty nail along where the binding glue held the silk cover in place. He tore it back, and inside was a piece of folded parchment. Calliope's mouth fell open.

The edge of the page was tattered, as if it had been torn hastily from another book in another time. Meredith pushed it across to the table.

A woman gazed up from the page. She was dressed in crimson silk, a crown of pearls resting atop a heap of onyx curls. Her lips curved into a gentle smile, lifted by high, honied cheeks that flushed rose pink at their crest. Hazel eyes laughed at Calliope, bright and clear as if they were real rather than painted, and in her hand, she held a shining golden feather.

Calliope stared down at the woman, a chill spreading over her. She looked up and across to the glass behind Meredith's chair where her own face reflected back. The same curls, the same eyes, the same crooked mouth.

Calliope's mind suddenly felt the way it did when she first woke in the morning, all blurry, caught in the half-world between dreams and consciousness. "She looks like me."

Meredith swallowed, nodding slowly. "She was your mother." He cleared his throat. "The Queen of Lyrica."

Calliope shook her head, trying to understand what Meredith was saying. She noticed the title at the corner of the piece of parchment. *The Firebird Queens: A History of Lyrican Royal Lineage.* Of course, she had read about the Firebird Queens before, but Meredith had never brought her a book that showed what any of the Queens actually looked like. Now she knew why.

She shook her head, trying to get her brain to work properly. If her mother had been the Firebird Queen, then that made all the stories she'd read about Lyrica real.

"You lied to me," she croaked.

"No! I would never. I—" Meredith broke off, rubbing at his face, pulling at his cheeks like he was trying to rearrange his own features. "I thought it would be easier for you to be happy if you didn't know. Being the Princess doesn't mean what you might think."

Calliope jumped to her feet. "All my life I've accepted that this is the way things are. I've been good and stayed put just like you told me! Don't you think I wanted to come with you? Don't you think I hated being alone? Now you tell me that my mother was the *Queen of Lyrica*? Why would you keep that from me? Why?"

It felt cruel that she had read so many tales about Lyrica and her Queens without ever knowing that they were a part of her own story.

Meredith sighed. "Calliope, please calm down."

She shook her head. "Tell me *why*."

Meredith cleared his throat. "I wanted you to be safe." His

fingers drummed the table for a moment before he clenched them tight. "Calliope, your mother was murdered, and the woman responsible—the Spectress—wants you dead, too. She will do anything to find you. She has torn babies from their parents' arms in search of you."

Calliope hugged herself, a rushing sound in her ears. "Why?" she said. "What did I do?"

Meredith looked around as if he might find the answer beneath the window seats or in the driftwood chandelier.

Finally, he spoke. "Do you remember the story of the first Firebird Queen?"

Calliope nodded.

Meredith folded his hands on the table, his knuckles white. "The legend says that it was the girl's perfect hope that drew the Firebird back. She remembered 'The Firebird Song' when no one else had, not even the Ancient Spirits. She had done the impossible and ended the Demon's reign of fear. Because of her, the Demon was trapped beneath the earth.

"The Firebird rewarded her with a Feather plucked from its own tail and promised her this: her ancestors would always have the power to call it back. Once they reached the Age of Hope, if they still remembered its Song and held the Feather in their hands, it would return.

"But that is not the end of the story. The Demon's memory is eternal. For a thousand years, he has dreamed of nothing but vengeance. He has bided his time, searching for a servant who could wield his power."

"The Spectress," whispered Calliope. The name felt strange and serpentine on her tongue.

Meredith nodded. "Yes. He uses her as a vessel, giving her terrible power so he might rid the world of hope and be free once and for all."

Calliope pulled her curls, trying to make sense of what he was saying. "But if I'm the daughter of a Firebird Queen, then I can call the Firebird, too, can't I? Except—" She sat back down at the table. "I don't know the Song. Do you?"

Meredith shook his head. "Only the Firebird Queens knew the Song. It was passed down from generation to generation. Truthfully, I'm not sure there was all that much magic left in the Song anyway. Maybe it still would have worked, the Song and the Feather together, but I don't know. We had forgotten the real meaning of it. It's there in our stories, but that's all we thought they were."

Calliope chewed her lip. She understood completely. After all, she had read many books about the Firebird Queens, but until now, they had all been fairy tales. "Maybe if you give me the Feather, I'll remember the Song on my own." She held out her hand.

Meredith shook his head. "The Feather was stolen."

Her heart sank. "Stolen? Who would do such a horrible thing?"

Meredith sighed. "We didn't even realize it was missing—not until it was too late. The Thief had already disappeared without a trace."

"But it must be out there somewhere," said Calliope. "It couldn't just vanish."

She jumped to her feet, running and grabbing Meredith's arm. "Let's go! Let's find it!" She bounced on her toes. "I'm the Age of Hope! That's what you were waiting for, isn't it? That's why you didn't tell me until now. You knew the Song wouldn't work until I reached the Age of Hope!" Calliope beamed at him.

Meredith's mouth turned down behind his mustache. "No, Calliope, you can't leave. You are in more danger than ever. The Spectress knows that you have come into your power. She will expect you to go looking for the Feather."

"I don't care!" said Calliope, suddenly furious. "She murdered my mother! Doesn't that make you angry? Don't you want to stop her?"

Meredith blinked. "Of course, but it's never wise to act in anger, Calliope. It clouds your vision and makes you reckless." He pointed at the window. "Look. Go on."

Calliope did. Her cheeks were splotchy and her round nose was red.

"Nothing has changed, not really. The Age of Hope hasn't made you grown-up." Meredith crumpled his hat between his hands. "Someday, your time will come. You'll be ready. But we can't risk it now. You're still just a girl, and I can't let anything happen to you. Lyrica needs you alive. You're the only hope we have left."

With that, Meredith tipped the hourglass back over and

slipped beyond the door, leaving Calliope to stare at her own face in the glass.

Still just a girl.

She had thought she'd heard him say it for the last time, thought that today would be the day that everything changed, but gazing at her reflection, even she had to admit that she didn't look any different.

Still, how could she stay now that she knew the truth about who she really was? How could she keep hiding knowing that she might be the only one who could save Lyrica? Knowing that people were being hurt and killed beyond her door?

No. Calliope sat up straighter, tilting her chin at her reflection. She had to try—even if she had to do it all alone.

Before she could lose her nerve, she grabbed a satchel and carefully tucked the folded portrait of her mother inside before tossing Meredith's book back in its place.

She stuffed an extra set of clothes, her new book, a pair of shears, some parchment, and a box of ancient matches she'd found in an old chest into the bag; then she snatched Brown Bear, Hippo, and Lion and stomped toward the door.

Calliope took a deep breath and shoved it open. She stood for a moment, staring out at the world on the other side of the threshold.

Everything was a mystery beyond the door, and if what Meredith had told her was true, it would be dangerous.

It wasn't too late; she could change her mind. She could shut danger out and stay safe in the world she knew.

You're still just a girl.

"Princesses don't hide from dangerous things no matter *how* young they are," she argued aloud. She didn't care what Meredith said—she would be the kind of princess who stood up to scary things, even if it meant she might get hurt.

So with the entire, uncertain world ahead and everything safe and familiar at her back, Calliope stepped over the threshold at last.

6

Prewitt hurried down the city steps, trying not to slip on the thick coating of mud.

A small boy in a too-big waterman's jacket hunched on the steps below. Prewitt called out, "Jack!"

Jack turned, and his round face dimpled. "Firebird feathers! I almost didn't recognize you in that jacket. You look just like the Bargemaster!"

Jack's lap was a mass of nets, and his black braid poured rain. Prewitt knew he'd probably been there for hours. There were cracks in the dark skin on Jack's knuckles and they looked painful, but Prewitt had never heard the other boy complain.

He looked down at the smelly nets, biting his lip, and on impulse he said, "I want to tell you something, but I need to know that you can keep a secret."

Jack tilted his head, and his brown eyes were clear as he

held the backs of three fingers to his lips. "Waterman's Word. You can trust me," he said. "What is it?"

Prewitt copied him solemnly, looking back over his shoulder to make sure they were alone. "The Lost Princess is alive."

Jack didn't react the way Prewitt had expected. He didn't jump up or pepper him with questions. Instead, his head bowed back over the nets, and his fingers returned to their work.

"Didn't you hear what I said?"

Jack nodded. "I heard." He was still trying to process Prewitt's words. They had sent an explosion of emotions through him. Hope, doubt, and fear all ricocheted around his heart at once, and he didn't know what to feel. "Are you sure?" he said finally.

"Yes! She's the Age of Hope today, and that means she can call the Firebird back and defeat the Spectress. I have to find her."

Jack blinked at him. "How?"

"I'm going to take the *Queen's Barge* upriver. I'll search every town if I have to."

"Alone?"

Prewitt crouched down. "I thought maybe you'd want to come with me. You know more about boats than I do."

Jack's forehead furrowed, and rain dripped from his brows. "I can't, Prewitt. I'm not brave like you."

Prewitt's gut twisted. If Jack knew the truth, if he knew that he'd run away instead of facing the ash golems, he would never have called him brave.

Jack shook his head. "What if you're wrong? What if the Spectress catches you?"

Prewitt scowled. "Firebird feathers, Jack, I thought you would *want* to help! After what they did to your parents! Don't you even care?"

Jack's head dropped back over the nets. "I'm really busy, Prewitt," he mumbled. How could he explain that it was *because* of his parents that he couldn't take risks? They had died while he had lived, and Jack wouldn't take that for granted.

Prewitt shifted awkwardly from foot to foot. He regretted telling Jack about the Princess. He had been so certain that the other boy would understand, that he'd want to help. "You won't tell anyone, will you?"

Jack looked up at him, unblinking. "I gave you the Waterman's Word. I would never break that."

Prewitt felt a pang. After all, hadn't he given his father the Waterman's Word only the night before? He pressed his hands into his pockets as if he could somehow tuck the guilt away.

Prewitt swallowed. "I guess . . . I guess I'll just see you later then."

Jack didn't answer as Prewitt continued on down the steps.

The tide was starting to come in, but Prewitt had gone only a few feet before he hesitated, turning back.

"I shouldn't have said that about your parents," he said, the words tight in his throat. Jack smiled, but his eyes were sad. "If I knew we would find her, I would help you, Prewitt, really I would. I think if I knew that for certain she was alive, I could have courage to do something brave. But what if you're wrong? What if she died all those years ago, just like we thought?"

"Then at least I did *something*," said Prewitt.

"Sometimes keeping your head down and doing your best to stay alive *is* doing something," said Jack, but even as he said it, he didn't truly believe it.

Prewitt climbed over driftwood and crunched across broken shells and bottles, doing his best to avoid the slimy, rotting fish. He saw a pearl mixed with the mess, but he didn't bother to pick it up. Once, a pearl had been worth a fortune, but now, there was nothing left of value to buy.

He stood on the Bookshop stoop in full view of the marauders. If they looked down, they might see his red jacket through the fog. He wished he hadn't worn it.

There was a loud crack and a splash, followed by a barrage of swearing. "There goes another mast!" He heard the rough voices of fishermen and knew they were close, but he couldn't see them through the murk that blanketed the black sea.

He turned back. The half-moon window in the Bookshop door was boarded over. He took a deep breath and knocked.

He grew more and more anxious as he waited, and he looked up, trying to see through the windows higher up, but they were covered in mist.

He knocked again, this time louder, standing on his tiptoes and peering through the gap between the boards.

An eye stared back at him.

Prewitt yelped and nearly fell off the stoop.

"You shouldn't be here," said a low voice. The eye blinked behind half an oval spectacle. Its iris was a light, almost translucent blue, a stark contrast to the red-streaked whites that surrounded it.

"I'm looking for the Bookkeeper," said Prewitt.

"Dangerous pastime these days."

"Please," said Prewitt, looking over his shoulder. "Will you let me in?"

"Can't you read?" The eye flicked to the side, and Prewitt saw a sign tied to a rusting nail.

He squinted at it, trying to sound out the words. "C-C—"

"Emperor's gut!" sputtered the man, and the eye vanished. There was a loud *click* of a bolt being thrown, then a sound like a chain being drawn back, then more *click*s and *clack*s all in quick succession. The door inched open, and a large nose poked through. "It says Closed Indefinitely. Have we really come to a time when the Bargemaster's own son can't read?"

Prewitt bit his lip, his cheeks hot. His mother had started teaching him, helping him trace letters in a plate full of sand, but after the book was taken, she had dumped the sand onto the muddy tier outside their house.

The door creaked open. "Hurry up, then. We don't have much time. The tide will soon be in."

Prewitt glanced over his shoulder and then slipped inside. He recognized the man before him at once. The spotted head, the bent back.

"Follow me, and stick to the shadows," said the Bookkeeper. "Don't speak until we pass through the atrium."

After he'd come and taken all the books away, the Bookkeeper had locked himself in the shop. If someone spied his face in one of the windows, they did not speak of it for fear that a marauder would hear and accuse them of curiosity and book hunting and send them off the cliffside.

Now the Bookkeeper pressed himself warily against the shelves and side-shuffled around the atrium, staying out of the lantern's red light.

After a moment's hesitation, Prewitt followed.

The floor was covered in dirty water that dripped down from the cracked sea-glass dome high above. Crimson shadows flickered around the shop, and he shivered as his eyes ran across the rotting shelves. Mold and cobwebs swelled like shrouds where books had once been. White marble steps wound to the top of the dome, streaked with grime and bright green algae.

The Bookkeeper's dirty slippers slapped across the atrium, and Prewitt hurried to catch up. They reached a thick curtain, and the Bookkeeper heaved it to the side.

Prewitt pushed through, and the curtain slumped back into place. The room was dark but for a stream of red light that spilled through a tear in the curtain and trickled across the floor.

The ancient Bookkeeper shuffled to sit on a low bed nearly hidden in the shadows. It creaked and rocked, and for a moment, Prewitt thought he saw something gold shimmering beneath it, but his attention was drawn away when the Bookkeeper spoke.

"What brings you to my Bookshop, Bargeboy? As you can see, I'm running rather low on inventory these days."

Prewitt ran a hand through his hair. "A long time ago, you came and took a book from our house. It was gold with—"

"With red lettering embossed on the front. Yes, I remember," snapped the Bookkeeper. "I remember all the books and all the names of anyone who has ever borrowed them. I remember the day your father asked for that book like it was this morning." He smoothed his scalp as if preening invisible hair. "He wanted you to know how things used to be. I think he viewed it as his own little rebellion."

Prewitt played with the buttons on his jacket. That didn't sound like his father to him. "Do you still have it?"

The Bookkeeper tilted his head. "My days of book smuggling are over, Bargeboy. Just as I remember all the books, I remember the deaths. I remember the sounds they made when the ash golems feasted on their flesh. Skin doesn't burn like paper, you know. It melts and drips like—"

Prewitt took a step backward, covering his ears, not wanting to hear. Granny Arila's face flashed in his mind. He knocked into a wooden chair beside a small desk, and a tiny silver pot toppled over, oozing thick black ink across water-wrinkled parchment. Prewitt rushed to clean it, but the Bookkeeper waved a gnarled hand. "Leave it."

Prewitt wiped his fingers on his pants. Above the desk, portraits of Bookkeepers past stared down at him with the same sharp eyes that watched him now. "I won't get caught," he promised. "I'll keep it secret. I'll be careful!"

"That's what they all said, and where are they now?"

"You don't understand—I *have* to have it. I *need* it."

The Bookkeeper's eyes glowed in the dark. "I understand perfectly."

Prewitt shifted beneath the Bookkeeper's suddenly piercing gaze.

"Today you reached the Age of Hope. It's a better day than most for a brave act—or a foolish one."

"How did you know?"

"I'm a collector of stories. What better tale than a Bargeboy and a Princess born under the same moon?"

Prewitt felt a jolt of synchronicity. Granny Arila had said nearly the same thing.

The Bookkeeper stood, and he came so close that Prewitt could feel the heat of his breath on his cheeks. "Tell me, Barge-boy, are you ready to risk everything you know, everything you love, even your own life, for what you seek?"

Prewitt swallowed. "Yes," he said, with more conviction than he felt.

The Bookkeeper grinned, and the effect was ghoulish in the red light.

"Then it's time. Follow me."

7

The old man cackled as he tottered to the end of the bed, running inky fingers across the metal bedstead and releasing a hidden latch. Prewitt sucked in a breath as the bed rotated away from the wall with a gentle clicking and whirring, revealing a circular golden hatch.

The Bookkeeper shuffled over to the hatch, reaching into the front of his robe and pulling out a silver chain. On it hung an ornate golden skeleton key. He turned toward Prewitt and winked, and Prewitt felt an ominous tickle at the base of his spine.

With a groan, the Bookkeeper bent down. The Queen's crest shone in sharp relief on the hatch, and the Bookkeeper pressed the key into the place where the feathers' two quills met. His hands were steady and sure as he turned it. He sat back on his haunches, and they both watched as gears turned, cogs spun, and tumblers clicked back. The branches of the apple tree twisted, and the hatch slid to the side with a musty sigh.

Cool air wafted from the tunnel below, and dim light curved up into the darkness, turning the Bookkeeper's face into a grinning skull.

"After you," he said, motioning Prewitt to the ladder that disappeared into the tunnel.

Prewitt swallowed.

"Unless you're more afraid than you've been letting on."

Prewitt shook his head, scowling. He sat on his bottom and slid until his legs dangled over the side of the hatchway. Once his boots found the metal rungs, he began the climb down, the light snatching at his toes. His feet slipped on the metal, and before he could catch himself, he tumbled down to the cool dirt floor.

Prewitt lay for a moment, dazed; then he pushed himself up, dusting off his jacket. He looked around as the Bookkeeper closed the hatch and climbed down after him, soggy slippers slopping on the rungs.

These were the tunnels, the ones he'd traced over and over again. The ones that led to the Sacred Cavern. Was that where the Bookkeeper was taking him? His father had said it was *impossible* to get into the tunnels, but here he was. He couldn't keep the grin from spreading across his face.

The walls of the tunnel gently luminesced, pulsing with a dim, otherworldly light, and Prewitt's eyes began to adjust.

To the left and right, the already narrow space was stacked floor to ceiling with books. They ran along the walls, piled on top of one another as far as Prewitt could see. "You hid them below the city?" he asked, amazed.

"As many as I could before the marauders descended like termites. Even then I'm afraid I could only save a fraction of the Shop." The Bookkeeper sighed and smoothed his fingers over his scalp and down his beard. "Come." He padded off, and Prewitt chased after him.

The tunnels wound in tortuous knots, each one the same as the last, and Prewitt was glad the Bookkeeper knew his way. It would be far too easy to get lost down here without a map.

Damp gray rock curved to meet more damp gray rock. And more, and more, and more, until suddenly, the Bookkeeper stopped.

"Here we are," he said in a reverent whisper. He ran his fingers across colorful book spines, selecting a particularly thick volume and sliding it gently from the stack.

Prewitt's shoulders slumped. "I thought maybe you were taking me to the Barge."

"The Barge? Now, where would you get an idea like that? You said you were looking for your maps."

Prewitt bit his lip, flushing. "I am."

The Bookkeeper leaned close, holding out the book, and Prewitt could smell his breath, musty and sweet. The Bookkeeper pulled back the cover with painstaking slowness, as if not wanting to disturb a creature that lay between the pages.

The book had been hollowed out, and nestled within was a small black conch shell.

"You came searching for your maps, but what I am about to give you is far more valuable." The Bookkeeper caressed the shell with a finger.

"There is a legend of a rift between the Ancient Spirits. Most believe it to be just another fairy tale, but I have never been so certain. The legend said that the rift was the result of a prophecy that no human ear had ever heard, one that told of great doom. It said that rather than stay to see the prophecy played out, the Spirits chose to flee across the sea."

Prewitt glanced up. Granny Arila had mentioned a prophecy, too. He had wondered what she meant, but there hadn't been time to ask.

The Bookkeeper's eyes glittered. "As a man with a thirst for knowledge, I always wondered where they could have gone. Can you think of a place across the ocean where no Lyrican has tread and returned?"

Prewitt shook his head. He was getting more and more spooked by the moment.

"Where else but the Nymph Isles?" said the Bookkeeper. "Magical gifts have arrived from the Isles for Queens throughout the ages, and yet no one has ever seen who delivered them. The Isles have never sent an envoy, nor have they allowed one to step foot on their shores. It all made me wonder."

Prewitt could picture the Nymph Isles in his mind's eye, floating like crescent moons at the top of the page of seas.

"I spent years searching texts for anything that could support my surmising. I scoured collections across the kingdom, including the most ancient library in all of Lyrica, in the dark heart of the mountains. I collected as much knowledge as I could, always wondering if my obsession was merely a fool's pastime.

"But after the Spectress joined the Demon, I knew the time had come. You see, there is only one creature who can stop the Demon once its power has been unleashed—our Firebird. The Ancients knew this, but they also knew that the Firebird had given the Queen the power to call it back at any moment, and the first Queen was still young and vibrant when they fled the kingdom.

"No, something else frightened them. Something about our future that they had kept to themselves. So after the Terrible Thing, I took a ship and set out, determined to sacrifice anything necessary to get answers."

The Bookkeeper's glassy gaze settled on the conch. "I paid a great price for this shell. A price many would judge. But what price is too high for knowledge?"

Prewitt shivered.

"Are you ready, Bargeboy? Ready to hear what years of study and a willingness to sacrifice purchased me?"

Prewitt looked up, suddenly understanding. "The prophecy. You found it!"

"Yes," hissed the Bookkeeper. "I succeeded where no one before me had ever even dreamed. I have heard what no human besides myself has ever heard. I have heard the *future*." He reached down and grasped the shell. "It's how I knew that one day, you would come."

The Bookkeeper thrust the shell at Prewitt. Its surface shone like poison in the dim light.

Prewitt took another step backward. "I only came for my book."

"And you shall have it, but first, you will receive the knowledge that the Ancients hid from us. *You will listen.* It is the price I demand for your book."

Prewitt chewed the inside of his cheek. What choice did he have? Holding his breath, he reached out and took the shell. It was smooth and cool and fit snugly in the palm of his hand, and before he could change his mind, he pressed the lip to his ear.

At first, he heard only the sound of the sea, a familiar drone, and then came the voices. They spoke in an eerie chorus, and Prewitt had to strain to hear above the Bookkeeper's ragged breath.

Hope will shatter, fear will rise
Twelve years to burn
Twelve years to die

Twelve years to suffer
Twelve years of hate
The Demon's Mark will seal our fate

Stones will bleed for what's been broken
Three slashes
Three tokens

Two sides
Once divided
Moon's halves must be united

For to a child our fates are tied
If from the ashes she does rise
If perfect hope she can achieve
Then all that's broke may be redeemed

But if she fails, then all will fall
Mankind and spirits one and all
Shall share the shroud of pain and shame
Endless sorrow, fear, and flame.

Prewitt stood, the shell pressed to his ear, unable to move or speak until the sea had drowned the voices once more. He shuddered, and his eyes flicked up. "It's just a bunch of scary riddles. It doesn't even make any sense."

"Prophecies rarely do before their fulfillment," said the Bookkeeper.

"But you said that this prophecy is how you knew I'd come. It didn't say anything about me at all."

"Did it not? *Moon's halves must be united.* Curious wording, don't you agree? Tell me: How old are you today? How long has it been since the Terrible Thing?"

Prewitt blinked. "Twelve years! Granny Arila was right! I *am* supposed to find the Princess." All the old woman's ramblings about the moon suddenly made sense.

The Bookkeeper's mouth broadened, and he was about to speak when a distant thudding made his bald head whip around.

He shoved Prewitt behind a stack of books, pressing his finger to his lips. Prewitt tried to give the shell back, but the Bookkeeper didn't take it.

"Keep it. You may need it." He reached over and slid a red volume from a nearby stack, handing it to him with a wink.

It was the book of maps. If Prewitt had been paying attention, he could have reached out and taken it himself.

Now, he hugged it close as he crouched behind the stacks, the sound of his heart seeming to echo around the walls as the thuds came closer.

Who else could be down in the tunnels?

The bootsteps turned the corner and halted. "Oh, Thomas! I wasn't expecting you down here. You usually wait for me in the Shop."

Prewitt sucked in his breath. He knew that voice. He peered between the stacks of books and felt suddenly sick.

His father was standing in the middle of the tunnel.

He had said there was no way in, had said it was too dangerous. Acid bubbled in Prewitt's gut, and his fury returned, raw and real. Was this where his father had been while Granny Arila was dying?

The Bookkeeper chuckled. "Oh, you know me, Bargemaster; just missing my little children. I like to check up on them every once in a while. Now, if you don't mind helping me back to the Shop, these old legs of mine aren't what they used to be, and I could use a hand climbing back up the ladder."

"Of course, Bookkeeper," said Prewitt's father, and the two men disappeared down the tunnel, chatting as they went.

Prewitt came out from behind the stacks. He stood for a moment, fighting the desire to chase after his father and demand to know why he had lied, but instead, he tucked the conch shell into his pocket and opened the book of maps.

He was going to do what he came to do. He was one half of the moon and the Princess was the other, and when it was all over, when the Spectress was defeated at last, he would face his father with his head held high, knowing that he, at least, had done the right thing when everyone else was too afraid.

He followed the map along the knotted passages, his nose buried in the page, but just as he had turned left around a particularly sharp curve, he bumped into someone.

He cried out, dropping the book, and when he looked up, he found himself face-to-face with a *girl*.

8

Calliope couldn't believe what she was seeing.

She had twisted, and turned, and wound her way through the tunnels until she finally decided that wherever she was going, she was definitely going the wrong way, when she rounded a corner and smacked headfirst into *someone*.

"Ow!" he cried, and it was definitely a *he*.

A boy, barely taller than she was, with messy brown hair and caramel-colored skin, smattered with a constellation of freckles. His cheeks were round and wind-burned, and he massaged his scrunched forehead with the palm of his hand, but when he saw her, his mouth fell open.

"Firebird feathers!" He rubbed his eyes. "Firebird feathers!" He said it again.

"Who are you?" asked Calliope, leaning down to pick up the fallen book. She held it out, but he went on staring.

"I'm Calliope," she tried. She nudged the book at him. It bumped his limp arm.

"But you—you're a girl!"

Calliope frowned, looking down at herself. "Of course I'm a girl."

"I've never seen a girl before! I mean—" The boy wrinkled his freckled nose. "I mean, I have *seen* girls, but I've never seen one *my age!*" His eyes widened. "Wait, how old are you?"

"I'm the Age of Hope today," said Calliope, standing a bit straighter. It felt good to tell someone. It made it more official.

Without warning, the boy let out a startling whoop and began twirling around the tunnel, punching his fists in the air. He knocked a book off a stack.

Calliope raised an eyebrow.

He grabbed her by the shoulders, shaking her. "You're *her!* I thought I'd have to search the whole kingdom, but—here you are!" He clutched something inside his pocket, his eyes wide. "I can't believe it. It's happening just like it says. I *knew* I was meant to find you!"

Calliope pulled away from him. "What are you talking about?"

"You're the Lost Princess, aren't you?"

Calliope scowled. She didn't know why, but there was something disconcerting about the fact that this boy knew she was a princess when she hadn't known herself until an hour ago. "You haven't told me who *you* are," she said.

"I'm Prewitt." He gave a little bow. "The Royal Bargeboy." Prewitt looked Calliope up and down. She wasn't what he had expected at all.

She was scrawny, and the top of her head barely reached his chin. She wore pants covered in bright patches, and she had tucked strange paper figures into a light-pink sash that cinched the waist of an enormous shirt. Too-long sleeves were rolled and pinned with ornate jeweled brooches.

"I was looking for you," he said. "Well, actually, I was looking for the *Queen's Barge*, but only because I was trying to find you!"

Calliope smiled. "Then you would have found me soon enough anyway. The Barge is my home!"

Prewitt listened as Calliope told him about finally working up the courage to leave the Cavern. "Mer told me to stay where I was safe, but how can I when there's something I can do? He says the Age of Hope doesn't change anything but—" She broke off, catching Prewitt's expression. "Is something wrong?"

"What did you say the man's name was?" But he knew. It all made sense now: the long absences, his father's adamant refusal to take him to the Barge. He had been protecting *her*.

"Meredith. Why? Do you know him?" asked Calliope.

Prewitt's heart clenched like a fist. "He's my dad."

"Mer never told me he had a son." Calliope frowned. "I guess he never told me a lot of things."

The children stood in the tunnel, tangled in a web of shared emotion.

Finally, Calliope spoke. "Well, we've found each other, and whether Meredith likes it or not, we're going to find the Feather, too."

"You don't have it?" asked Prewitt.

"No, it was stolen. But I'm sure you and I can get it back," said Calliope.

"Can't you just sing the Song without it?"

Calliope's cheeks reddened. "I don't know the Song," she admitted.

Prewitt rubbed the back of his neck. "Okay, so we'll find the Feather, and then we'll figure out the Song. How hard can it be?" He flipped through his book until he reached the page that showed the Cavern, tracing his finger along the lines of the tunnels.

"If we work together, I'm sure we can find a way to launch the Barge; then we can search the cities along the river. Someone is bound to have seen something."

He chewed on his lip. "We'll have to be careful, though," he said. "Somehow, the Spectress has convinced the Falconer to help her. She has something he wants. I don't know what, but if his birds see us, we're done. Actually, now that I think about it, it's probably safer if you just stay hidden on the Barge and let me do the searching—"

"I'm not going back to the Barge," interrupted Calliope. "I'm going here." She flipped the page and tapped her finger against the castle.

"The Cursed Castle? No way. That's the last place we should go."

"Why?"

"Because the marauders watch it all the time. Not only that, but it's where the Terrible Thing happened. It's where your parents—" He cut himself off, not wanting to say it out loud.

"But what if my mother left me a clue?" said Calliope. "She wouldn't have just sent me into hiding with nothing at all! She must have known I'd need the Song someday."

Prewitt shook his head. "The ash golems burned everything. Even if she did leave a clue, it couldn't have survived. There was nothing left after the Terrible Thing except . . . except . . ." He suddenly remembered Granny Arila's story. *The strangest thing of all were the words scrawled across the nursery wall.*

Calliope's nose was an inch from his. "What? What is it? Tell me!"

The words were barely out of his mouth before she was yanking him down the tunnel.

"They might not even be there anymore," he protested.

"They will be!" Calliope slowed as they reached another turn. She frowned. She'd never had to worry about things like directions in the Sacred Cavern. "You lead," she said.

They walked for a while, turning, sloping, slanting, until they found a ladder similar to the one Prewitt had climbed down from the Bookshop except much longer.

Calliope grabbed the rungs and began to climb, but Prewitt hesitated. "I have a bad feeling about this," he said.

"I don't," said Calliope, and before he could argue further, she shoved the hatch open and heaved away the corner of a heavy, soot-stained rug. She coughed and choked as she pulled herself out of the hatch and into a damp cloud of dust and ash.

She crawled onto crackling carpet and knelt for a moment, taking in the room. Dim green light and rain poured through what remained of a high, arched window, and water cascaded down shards of broken glass, sending shadows like skeletal hands raking across her pants legs.

She pressed her palm across her nose as she took in the charred nursery. Her eyes burned with the harsh stench of soot. A sea-glass chandelier rattled in a bent frame overhead, and in the shadows, a toy castle slumped into a heap.

She squeezed her eyes shut and tried to imagine the nursery as it had been before, her mother standing near the bed.

Calliope wished desperately that she had a memory of her. Her scent, her voice, her touch. Just one thing she could hold on to. Something that might make her real. What would it have felt like to be in her arms? To be loved? But no matter how she tried, she couldn't escape the ghosts of tragedy that still haunted the ravaged room. She had thought seeing the nursery would make her feel closer to her mother, but instead, she felt more alone than ever.

A hand on her shoulder made her jump, but she let out her breath when she saw Prewitt's freckled face peering at her. "Let's hurry so we can get out of here." He flicked a furtive glance at the window.

Calliope got to her feet, dusting off her pants. She shivered.

The cool air was filled with floating motes of dust and ash, suspended as if time had ceased forever within the four walls of the nursery.

"Cal, look!" Prewitt tiptoed across the singed rug toward the rusted bed frame. The dirty remains of a tattered canopy swept toward him like the tentacles of an octopus, and Calliope wanted to shout out a warning, but instead she calmed her voice and said primly, "It's Calliope—not Cal."

"Okay, but look!" Prewitt pointed to a stone planter that stood on the side of the bed near the door. It overflowed with trumpet-shaped white flowers and green vines that twisted up around the decrepit bed frame.

A draft swept around the room, and the sweet scent of the blossoms mixed with the acrid smoke.

The chandelier rattled, the canopy whispered, and the flowers bobbed their heads as if to say, "So you've come at last."

Calliope sneezed.

"I've never seen flowers before," whispered Prewitt. "I wonder what kind they are." A cloud of moths swarmed up out of the blooms. He batted them away and shook out his coat sleeves to make sure none of the insects had been trapped there. He flushed, glancing over to see if Calliope had seen him overreact, but she wasn't paying attention.

She hovered over a bassinet in the corner. The little basket leaned perilously, cocooned in molding satin and torn, damp gauze. She wrapped her arms around herself, letting her gaze drift up across the walls.

"The words are supposed to be written on the wall," whispered Prewitt. "But I don't see them anywhere."

A portrait hung above a large fireplace. Paint bled down the Queen's and King's melted faces, and their eyes shone ghastly white. Calliope's eyes hurried on, her heart thrumming.

"If only we had more light!" She stomped her foot. She had never been in this kind of gloom. She suddenly remembered the matches in her bag. She reached down, opening her satchel and pulling out the matchbox. *Please*, she begged, *please help me find something.*

She struck a match on the side of the box, holding it up to a cracked and dirty mirror hanging beside the fireplace. For a moment, the light glowed against her face, brightening her reflection, and then she saw it. Visible for just a moment as a low breeze caught the canopy.

Calliope turned, moving forward in a daze, holding the match gingerly between her fingers.

Prewitt had crawled under the bed, searching, and she stepped over his outstretched legs without a word.

He frowned as he felt the light change, the shadows beneath the bed stretching and flickering in the new, warmer light. "Cal? What are you doing?"

She didn't answer. Instead, she reached out her hand, pulling aside the canopy. The wind snatched the flame, and the match went out, casting them back into darkness. Calliope fumbled with the matchbox.

This was it. She knew it. She was about to see what her mother had left her.

Prewitt wriggled his way out from under the bed. He looked up, catching the way Calliope's fingers shook as she slid open a small box and drew out a thin wooden stick. For a moment, Prewitt wasn't sure what it was. But when she struck it on the side of the box and a flame erupted from the tip, he shouted.

"Don't!" He barreled toward her, knocking the match out of her hand. Sparks showered across the carpet. He stomped on them with his boots, trying to stifle them before they could ignite, but it was no use. The more he stomped, the more they multiplied, hopping like demon beetles across the charred fibers. They snatched the gauze canopy, and before Prewitt knew it, the fabric was ablaze.

It whipped and lashed, and Prewitt flinched away.

Calliope was too absorbed to notice Prewitt's fear, for in the firelight, the words on the stone were clear at last. "My mother's message. I found it!" She reached up a hand, pressing her fingers to the writing that was finally visible in the light of the burning canopy. It was hastily scrawled, diminished by age and damp, but it was there, and for a moment, with her hand against the cool stone and the warmth from the flames lapping at her back, Calliope was certain that she felt her mother's presence.

Wind. Woman. Thief.

Just three words.

"Cal, please, we have to go!" choked Prewitt, reaching forward to pull Calliope away, but she shook him off.

"My mother was here, Prewitt; don't you see? She was here!

75

She left this message for me!" The firelight glowed across the writing, illuminating the dark rust color of them, the shadows rippling so that the words seemed to drip down the wall like . . . like . . .

Calliope stumbled back, her foot pressing down on something sharp. It cut through her heel, blood instantly blossoming over the carpet. Looking down, she saw shards of black glass, flickering like oil across the floor.

She clapped a hand to her mouth, eyes welling. "It's blood! She wrote the words in blood!"

Prewitt hadn't paid attention before, too caught up in his own fear to care about the message. But now he saw the way the words dripped down the wall, almost as if the stones themselves were bleeding. His hand went to his pocket. *Stones will bleed for what's been broken.*

The flames snapped, and he shook off the prophecy, reaching for Calliope's hand. "We don't have time for this. We have to get out of here before—"

But it was too late. The ash golem was already forming, billowing up from the sizzling canopy. It grew upward, expanding until its head pressed against the ceiling, a monster of magma and ash.

Calliope stared up at it, horrified. Was *this* the last thing her mother had seen? Was this how she had died? She had wanted a memory of her mother, had wanted a way to feel close to her, but this—this was terrible.

Smoke clung to the monster like cobwebs, its gaping black

mouth a yawning hole. Where eyes should have been, there were only hollow sockets, but Calliope knew it was watching her. It roiled and shifted, whirling and writhing, molten veins throbbing and pulsing as it leaned toward her.

"Cal! We have to go—*now!*"

Calliope tore her eyes away and hurled herself down the ladder.

Prewitt followed, stopping only to slam the hatch shut with an earsplitting *bang*.

They dropped down into the tunnel, both breathing hard.

"I don't understand," said Calliope. "What—what was that thing?"

Prewitt's fear spewed from him in a torrent. "What's so hard to understand? You started a fire and almost got us killed, and for what? For some pointless message I already told you about!"

Prewitt shook his head, and his cheeks were hot. "It wasn't supposed to be like this. You were supposed to have the answers. You were supposed to give everyone hope and make things better, but you don't know *anything* at all."

The look on Calliope's face made Prewitt instantly regret his words, but there wasn't time to apologize. For at that very moment, they saw it:

A single spark clinging to Prewitt's boot.

They ran. On and on they raced, winding through the labyrinth. Prewitt's head bent over the book of maps, praying that he was reading it correctly, hoping that they were leaving the ash golem far behind.

They turned a corner, and without warning, the tunnel widened, the rock vaulting overhead, and there they were, lodged in the rock in front of them, a gold door just like in his book.

Prewitt ran forward.

Calliope's shoulders slumped. To her, the door felt like failure.

Prewitt pushed on the door, but it didn't budge.

Calliope stepped forward. "I have to do it," she said, and with a gentle shove, she pushed the door open and they slipped inside.

Flames gnashed like teeth, and Prewitt yelped, throwing up an arm to protect himself. "They got in!" he shouted.

"No," said Calliope. "No, it's okay." She reached up and pulled Prewitt's hand from his eyes. "Don't be afraid. We're safe here. Fire is different in the Cavern. I didn't know." Calliope stepped forward, holding her palms toward the blazing brazier. It turned them orange, but no monsters appeared.

"I'm not afraid," snapped Prewitt, shoving himself away from the door, but he stayed far from the flames as he took in his surroundings, searching, searching for what he'd dreamed of seeing for as long as he could remember.

His eyes traveled across the intricate sea-glass floor and out over a long dock, and then he saw her.

Floating at the end of the dock, moored to silver bollards, was the *Queen's Barge*.

9

Prewitt stood at the edge of the sprawling atrium, trying to calm his heart so he could let the moment soak in. He had imagined it so many times.

She floated serenely on the surface of a black lake that stretched farther than the light reached. A massive firebird figurehead curved up from the prow, better than any drawing. It flickered gold, and sparkling ruby eyes flashed in the torchlight. Gilded wings wrapped aft around the hull, thousands of intricate feathers shining amber in the glow of enormous lanterns swaying from the golden gunwale. Painted oars jutted out from decorated rowlocks, blades poised to plunge into the water at the Bargemaster's command, and at the center of the quarterdeck rose an ornate golden carriage.

Above it all, suspended at the very top of the poop deck, was a beautiful golden fog bell. An eight-pointed star shimmered at its center, radiant in the firelight, and the starry buttons on Prewitt's jacket flashed in response.

Prewitt felt suddenly as if his entire life up until then had been the drawing, flat and motionless, and now, at last, he was stepping off the page and into something real, something magical. The Barge was even more—

Calliope sucked in her breath.

Prewitt jerked his head toward her. His eyes followed her horrified gaze down to the shimmering tiles. A single orange spark sizzled and skittered, a toe's breadth from his boot.

"One got in!" she whispered. "I didn't think it could."

Their eyes met, and they fled toward the Barge, Prewitt's boots pounding, Calliope's soles slapping, and both their hearts thumping them frantically onward.

Calliope glanced over her shoulder. The monster was rising, its smoke-black shadow swelling up, blotting out the glow of the brazier. It stretched undulating limbs out across the Cavern like a living nightmare.

Her fingers fluttered at her sash, feeling for Lion's reassuring mane, for Hippo's bow, for Brown Bear's glasses as she ran onward, up the gangplank. She leaped over the gunwale.

"There has to be something we can do!" She searched desperately for anything that might be helpful. If only Meredith were there! For the first time, she wished she had listened to him. He had been right. She *was* just a girl. How could she ever hope to defeat monsters like these?

Through the carriage window, she saw the hourglass, still

sitting where Meredith had last tipped it over. She burst through the door, snatched it up, then ran back out to the row deck.

Prewitt had sat down on the dock, fumbling with his boots.

"What are you doing?" she screamed. "Get up here!"

"I can't. Not with my boots on!" Prewitt couldn't keep the panic from his voice as he struggled with his laces. "It's bad luck!"

Calliope slapped a hand to her forehead. "Leave them! Bad luck won't matter in a moment!"

The ash golem was fully formed now, a shifting black giant writhing across the Cavern.

Prewitt swallowed. It wasn't supposed to be like this. Not his first time on the Barge. He was the Bargeboy. There was a way to do things, and this wasn't it. Nothing was turning out the way he thought it would.

But Calliope was right; there wasn't time.

He jumped up, running forward and flinging himself over the railing just as the ash golem opened its fatal mouth. The heat of its breath seared the hairs on the back of his neck and flushed Calliope's cheeks crimson.

She flung the hourglass down, and it shattered, sending a shower of crystal and black sand across the deck. She looked to the golden doors, fully expecting Meredith to come running through at any moment, but before he could, she was knocked off her feet as Prewitt slammed into her.

They landed hard just as another burst of flames struck the deck.

But the golem's fire did not hurt them; instead, there was a blinding flash and the deck glowed bright white as a wave of water crashed across the hull in a gushing surge, dousing the light from the lanterns and dragging the Barge and the golem beneath the lake.

The oars clicked into their rowlocks as one, and a great bubble of air expanded all around. The golem slipped off the railing, falling back into the froth.

"What's wrong with it?" whispered Calliope.

A great glob of lava escaped the golem's grimace, hardening instantly in the cool water as the monster sank to the lake floor.

"It can't move," said Prewitt, as stunned as she was.

The rigid golem glared after them as the Barge rowed herself across the bottom of the lake.

It took a moment for their eyes to adjust as they left the Cavern's glow behind, but once they had, they found something new shining on the deck where the golem's breath had struck.

Calliope leaned down, her sopping curls sticking to her cheeks. "This wasn't here before." Goose bumps prickled her arms. A strange, luminescent symbol had appeared on the planks. She bent down, running her fingers across it. Two curving crescent moons were linked, one forward, one backward. One glowed pearlescent white, the other shone like wet slate. "What does it mean?"

Prewitt stared down at it. He knew exactly what it meant.

He turned to Calliope, his deep brown eyes shining; then he reached into his pocket and pulled out the black conch shell.

10

Prewitt and Calliope sat side by side on one of the ten row benches, a gentle draft drying their wet clothes and lifting Calliope's curls from her cheeks as they moved silently through the water.

Accompanied by the muffled strokes of the oars, Prewitt finally told her about going to find the Bookkeeper. He told her about the rift between the Ancient Spirits and about the prophecy that the Bookkeeper had gone all the way to the Nymph Isles to find.

When he was finished, Calliope pressed the conch shell to her ear. He watched her face as she listened, wondering what she was hearing and trying to read her thoughts. At last, she pulled it away and handed it back to him.

She stood and began to pace between the row benches. For a long time, she didn't speak, her feet padding to and fro across the planks. Finally, she came back and sat down.

"*Moon's halves must be united.* You think that is about us?"

Prewitt nodded. "That's what the Bookkeeper said. We were born on the same night. Granny Arila told me the same thing. She told me it was my destiny to find you."

Calliope frowned. "Who's Granny Arila?"

Prewitt grimaced. Why had he mentioned Granny Arila? He couldn't tell Calliope about the Singer, not without telling her what had *really* happened—that Prewitt had let Granny Arila send him away. He'd allowed his fear to keep him from helping his friend, from doing his duty as the Bargeboy, and she had died.

But Granny Arila had said his real duty was accepting his destiny, and that was helping the Princess. But Calliope would never trust him to help her call the Firebird back if she knew what a coward he'd been. He had to keep it a secret.

He changed the subject. "I figured out another part of the prophecy, too. The part about the stones. I realized it when we were in the nursery.

"*Stones will bleed for what's been broken,*" recited Calliope. "*Three slashes. Three tokens.*"

Prewitt nodded. "You were right, Cal. The words were written in blood."

Calliope nodded. She had known, but it still made her stomach twist. She couldn't think about it now. She had to think about the prophecy. "*Three slashes, three tokens.*"

"Three *words,*" said Prewitt.

"Three clues," whispered Calliope. "*Wind. Woman. Thief.*"

She frowned, trying to understand. "But what was broken? And what tokens?"

Prewitt shook his head. "I don't know."

Calliope stared out at the murky water. "So it really does all depend on me," she said. "But you heard the prophecy. If I fail, then—"

"You won't fail," said Prewitt. "I'm here. I'm the other half of the moon, and I'm not going anywhere. There's a reason that symbol appeared the moment we were both on the Barge. We're going to figure this out."

"But what about perfect hope? It says I have to have perfect hope. What does that even mean?"

Calliope tugged her curls, and Prewitt wished he knew the answer.

Calliope jumped up. "Enough wondering. Come on."

She marched down the aisle toward the carriage, stepping around the mess of sand and shards from the broken hourglass. Had Meredith found the broken glass in his pocket? Had he come to the Cavern? What would he think when he saw the Barge was gone?

"Where are you going?" asked Prewitt, catching up to her.

"To find answers."

The carriage was piled with books, scattered around the floor and across the window seats. Only a long wooden table at the center of the carriage was clear of them.

"Now that we know the words have something to do with the tokens, we have a place to start."

Calliope arranged her paper animals in a row along the windowsill and started shuffling through books, opening and closing each before tossing them aside in a flurry. "The answers to almost everything can be found if you look in the right place." She glanced up, realizing that Prewitt hadn't joined her.

His eyes were fixed on three orbs set into brass stands at the center of the table.

"Haven't you seen storm glasses before?"

Prewitt tilted his head. He *had* seen them. Every boat in the harbor had its own storm glass. There was even an enormous one in the grimy window of the Drink's Bottom Tavern, but they were relics of a different time, when the sailors needed to know what weather would meet them on the open sea. The orbs warned of rising storms, but no one paid attention to them anymore. The weather never changed, and neither did the storm glasses. Masses of white crystals forever shrouded the glass, suspended like spirits in a liquid void, portents of an endlessly rising tempest.

But these storm glasses didn't make any sense. Although they were identical in shape and size, they each predicted something entirely different.

The first was familiar, clouded and murky, but in the next, the crystals pooled at the bottom, and the third was utterly black, no crystals, no liquid, just darkness. It gave him the creeps to look at it.

"Why are there three?" asked Prewitt. "And how can they all show different things?"

"One for the Barge, one for the Halcyon Glade, and one for the Nymph Isles." Calliope rattled them off without looking up from the page.

"The Halcyon Glade?" asked Prewitt. "I've never heard of that. It's not in my book."

Calliope didn't look up. "Of course not. No one knows where it is. It's a place humans can't go, just like the Nymph Isles. But at least we know where the Isles are. You could even sail there if you wanted; you'd just never return."

Prewitt rubbed his freckles. "The Bookkeeper did."

Calliope met his gaze. "I think he's probably the first," she said. She looked over at the third storm glass, full of darkness and nothing. "It never changes. Neither does the Halcyon Glade glass. It always shows sunshine."

Prewitt went to the table and picked it up, looking deep inside as if he might find answers within the pooling crystals.

Calliope went on. "The stories say the Halcyon Glade is where the Firebird dropped the seed from the Emperor's apple tree and all of Lyrica began. I think there was even a time when it was open to people, when all the spirits and humans lived together peacefully, but that was a long time ago. Now, it's hidden."

Prewitt had never heard that story. He looked around. There were so many books here. Had she read them all?

She turned back to the pages, flipping through them purposefully.

"What is it you're looking for exactly?" asked Prewitt.

"I'll know when I find it," said Calliope. "Something about wind, or a woman, or someone who might have had a reason to steal the Feather." She twisted her body, lifting up a stack of books and hefting them toward Prewitt. "Here, start with these and let me know if you find anything."

He hesitated, rubbing the back of his neck; then he took the books. He opened one and stared blankly at the page. "There aren't any pictures."

"Of course not. Words use up less space. It's your imagination that makes the pictures."

Prewitt looked down at the black scribbles swimming on the parchment.

Calliope continued flipping through books, but when she saw that he hadn't yet turned the page, she frowned. "What are you waiting for?"

He flushed. "I don't know how to read," he muttered.

Calliope stared at him. "You don't?"

Prewitt shook his head. The words he'd shouted at her in the tunnel flooded back to him in a shameful wave. *You don't know* anything *at all*. He was beginning to realize that he was the one who didn't know anything.

To Calliope's credit, she only shrugged. "It's all right. Why don't you look around? Maybe something else changed when we both got on the Barge together—like the symbol on the deck."

She went back to scanning books, tossing them aside one

after the other in rhythmic thuds, and Prewitt began to search for anything that might be helpful.

When he opened the arched door at the aft end of the carriage and stepped down into Calliope's cabin, his mouth fell open.

It wasn't the opulence that shocked him, although the cabin was the most beautiful room he'd ever seen. It was what Calliope had done to the room that made Prewitt gape.

The thick rug was almost completely hidden by intricate cutouts. Paper houses, trees, and animals of every possible kind were arranged around the room. Chains of flowers, birds, butterflies, and puffy clouds were strung from the low ceiling, and all around a metal bathtub, paper waves were strewn with sea creatures.

It must have taken her hours and hours to make all these things, and for the first time, Prewitt thought about how lonely she must have been, stuck in the Cavern for so long without anyone to talk to.

For some reason, Prewitt's mind went to Jack. Jack didn't have anyone, either, no family or friends, just Old Harry. All he had was work, going out early and returning late, head forever bent over a lapful of nets.

Maybe that was all a person could do—find purpose and make friends however they could—even if those friends were made of paper or rope.

Prewitt swallowed. Maybe that's why it had hurt so much when his book of maps had been taken away.

After a while, Prewitt gave up searching and climbed up to

the poop deck. He leaned out over the railing and skimmed his hands through the water.

A gentle *bawng* made Prewitt turn. The fog bell swayed and the star at its heart glittered.

Prewitt tugged on his buttons. He suddenly had the strange sensation that he had seen the star before—a long time ago.

Something nudged Prewitt's memory, and he reached into his jacket, pulling out his book. He opened it to the Royal City map, and there it was in the right-hand corner, floating above the tallest turret. Prewitt ran his fingers across it, and then he paused. There were words slanting beneath the star.

The door banged as he ran into the carriage. "What does this say?" he said, turning the book so Calliope could see.

She leaned forward. *"Our patron star shall guide us home, if hope can call it with a tone."*

"Patron star?" said Prewitt. "I've never heard of the patron star."

But of course, Calliope had. "It's the lodestar that helps sailors find their way back to the Royal City."

"What's a lodestar?" asked Prewitt, embarrassed. He hated asking so many questions, but he'd never even seen a star, not a real one. The sky was too covered in clouds for stars.

"A lodestar stays in a fixed place," said Calliope. "The sky moves all around with the seasons, but a lodestar never strays."

"How do you know all this?"

She shrugged. "It was in a book." She knew exactly which book, and it was the last one she wanted to look at now.

"What book? Show me!" Prewitt wondered how Calliope could be so nonchalant about things like books. If he had this many books, he would learn to read them all, and he would keep all the information in his head and be smarter than everyone else in the Royal City. Maybe even in the whole kingdom— except maybe the Bookkeeper. He had probably read every book that ever existed.

Calliope sighed, moving over to the desk. She didn't want to take the book out, didn't want to be reminded of Meredith's secrets. But she pulled open the drawer and lifted it out. Shining on the cover was Prewitt's eight-pointed star.

He ran his fingers across it and down to the words slanting beneath. "What does it say?"

"*Ancient Navigation: Spirits and the Seafarer.*" Calliope didn't have to look.

"What does it say about the star?" Prewitt fidgeted, wishing he could read it himself.

Calliope flipped the book open, thumbing through the pages, but before she had gotten to the one she was searching for, she stopped, sucking in a breath. "Prewitt, look!"

He bent forward, but the page she pointed at was black with words. "What? What is it? What does it say?"

"It's instructions," said Calliope. "For how to call the *Wind*."

11

"**This says that the Winds are four** of the Ancient Spirits and that they can be *summoned*."

Prewitt's eyes widened. "How?"

"Well, that's the thing. It isn't easy."

Prewitt sighed. "Of course not."

"First, there's a warning. It says: *Seafarer take heed, for like all spirits, the Winds do not like to be tamed, and each requires payment from those who would seek its assistance.*"

"Fantastic. So what'll it be, then? Firstborn child? Blood of a Bargeboy?"

"Be quiet and listen."

Prewitt pressed his lips together and made a motion as if he were locking them tight, tossing an invisible key over his shoulder.

Calliope went on. "*The East Wind demands a drowning, the*

South Wind trades in secrets, the North Wind steals your future, and the West Wind takes your past."

"What is it with all these riddles?" Prewitt exploded. "Can't anyone in this kingdom just write out a straightforward instruction?"

Calliope shrugged. "Some of it is sort of straightforward."

"What bit seems straightforward to you? The part about giving up your future or the one where it suggests you drown someone?"

"I'm beginning to think drowning you wouldn't be so bad," said Calliope, rolling her eyes.

"It's just so frustrating!"

"All we have to do is think it through for a moment. Half the Ancients won't help us. They left when they heard the prophecy, so there wouldn't be any point in calling them."

Prewitt nodded. "But which ones?"

Calliope tugged a curl. "The North Wind comes from the north. That's where the Nymph Isles are, so we probably won't get help from that one."

"Well, I don't want to give up my future," said Prewitt. "But my past hasn't been that great. I'd be glad to give that up." He thought about all the cold fish, about the rain, and mold, and loneliness. He thought about Granny Arila and then quickly pushed the thought away.

"I don't think you can give up just the bad things," said Calliope. "It probably takes the good things, too. Or maybe it *only* takes the good things and leaves you with all the bad."

Prewitt cringed. "Well, the only Winds left are the East or the South. A drowning or a secret."

Calliope looked at Prewitt.

"Don't get any ideas," he said, holding up his hands.

Calliope laughed. "Okay then, a secret."

"I don't have any secrets," said Prewitt a bit too quickly. His heart pricked, but he kept his face even. He wasn't that person anymore. What did it matter if he kept it to himself?

Calliope tilted her head. "I suppose *I* count as a secret. Don't you?"

So, holding the Barge storm glass in her hands, Calliope stood at the prow, just behind the figurehead, staring out at the black water. Luminescent algae floated in great swaths, and the scent of brine filled her nostrils. Silver fish flashed.

Calliope shivered, sudden apprehension humming through her fingers, and for a moment, she wondered if she was making a mistake. What would Meredith say? She tossed her curls. He'd tell her to go inside, to wait for someone grown-up to do something.

But she didn't want to wait. She wanted to act. Her mother had written the words on the wall for her, had paid for them with blood, and she wasn't going to waste them.

She held the storm glass above her head and spoke out into the darkness.

"Ancient Spirit of the South Wind, I summon you with this secret. I am Calliope, the Lost Princess of Lyrica. I have been hiding for twelve years, but I hide no longer."

Prewitt stood behind her, skin prickling with the sudden energy of the moment. There was something new in Calliope's voice, something fierce and powerful. She seemed almost to grow as she spoke, and the orb glowed in her fingertips, the crystals within twisting into a swirling column.

The Barge hit a sudden current, and the children staggered. The water frothed white around them, and the Barge surged toward the surface, popping like a cork above the waterline.

Wind shrieked all around, and icy raindrops splattered their cheeks. They had emerged at the river, and the rapids raged, drenching them in angry spray. The oars continued their relentless strokes, fighting the current, struggling to keep the Barge steady against the wind that assaulted them.

"Show yourself, Spirit!" Calliope screamed, struggling to be heard over the din. She held the storm glass against her chest. It was slick with rain and river water.

The Wind howled back, and Calliope's feet slipped on the deck, but she was not deterred. "I am the Princess of Lyrica, and I command you to *show yourself!*"

Mist and rain gathered into a cyclone, spinning across the deck, and Calliope pressed her back against the railing. She watched as one of the benches was torn away, flung down into the river where it bashed against a rock before being devoured into the eddy.

Prewitt saw the silhouette of sharp cliffs rising ahead, and he knew that if the Wind's fury continued, the Barge would be bashed to pieces on the rocks.

"Calliope!" he shouted. But she did not hear him.

Her hair whipped her cheeks as the cyclone rushed closer.

It stopped inches before her toes, its tail ripping a hole in the deck. A splinter sliced across her cheek.

Here I am, Princess of Lyrica, last hope of her people.

Calliope did not falter. Her words were clear and confident. "I have heard the prophecy, have seen the blood on the stone. If you have a token, you must give it to me."

The Wind whirled for a moment, and then it said, *Why should I help you? Why should I assist the realm of humankind? They made a promise to protect what they'd been given, and that promise was broken. Why should I not leave you to your fate?*

Calliope felt anger rising within her. "I didn't ask for this! I didn't want to be hidden away in the dark, to be born into a doomed world! I'm just a girl, aren't I? I have every right to be as angry as you! Wouldn't I be justified if I stayed in the Cavern and let the world burn? I would have been safe. But I'm here, risking everything to set things right, to make up for sins that are not my own so that we can all have a chance at a life!"

The cyclone swayed slightly, then dissolved and re-formed, as if it were collecting its thoughts. *I feel something in you, Princess of Lyrica, something I have not felt for a thousand years. You do not hide from this battle like so many of my brothers and sisters. You face it willingly, knowing that you may lose, and for that, I will give you the token.*

It howled louder than ever and spun faster and faster until, at last, something appeared, bright and shining, at its core. The object rose and fell a few times before the cyclone broke apart, sending it spinning across the deck.

Calliope nestled the storm glass into the nearest row bench and bent to pick up the object. It was a small golden cylinder, a quarter inch wide, that glowed from within, illuminating shallow pins twining around the outer edges.

Prewitt stepped forward to see, but before he could get close, the Wind attacked, battering him from every side, pummeling with fist-like force.

Prewitt dropped to the deck, covering his face.

Coward, shrieked the Wind.

"I'm not!" cried Prewitt.

I can sense the secret festering within you, bystander.

Coward. Bystander. The words were rocks in a puddle, destroying the surface that Prewitt had tried so hard to keep smooth. His breath came in gasps as the Wind wrenched his hair and tore his jacket, and for a moment, Prewitt thought he heard Granny Arila's final scream in the wind. He pressed his palms to his ears. "No, please."

Prewitt couldn't bear it, couldn't hear the sound of her pain again.

Calliope dropped to her knees beside him. She shouted over the raging tempest. "Whatever it is, just say it! It can't be that bad."

Prewitt shook his head. "I can't. Once you know, you won't want me here anymore. But I'm the other half of the moon. I have to be here!"

The Wind grew angrier.

I will have what I am owed!

Two more benches tore from the deck, blankets and ropes drawn into the ravenous river. Glass shattered as one of the carriage windows was torn away.

The Barge veered suddenly starboard, and the hull smashed violently into the rocks.

"Prewitt!" shouted Calliope. "If you don't say it, we're going to crash! I promise I'll still want you here. We're friends, aren't we?"

Prewitt blinked, and the words scraped his throat, like a scab torn away. "It's my fault. Granny Arila died because of me. I should have kept her safe. I should have tried harder, but I didn't because I was afraid. I had a duty as the Bargeboy, and I failed." He was sobbing now, sobbing so hard, he didn't realize that the Wind had calmed.

I have been too harsh. The Wind's voice was no longer a shriek but a whisper against Prewitt's skin. *What I sensed was not quite a secret after all but remorse, which can fester all the same if kept within. I will take it from you.*

Prewitt wiped his cheeks, embarrassed, but somehow, speaking the truth out loud had eased the pain of guilt. He could feel his heart lightening.

Calliope hugged him tightly. "It's okay, Prewitt. It's over now."

Not quite. Now that I have taken your secrets, you must take one of mine.

Calliope and Prewitt glanced at each other. They weren't sure they wanted to carry one of the Wind's secrets. But before they could protest, the cyclone surrounded them entirely.

They were locked within it, spinning round and round, and they heard the strains of a tinkling, metallic tune drifting up and around them.

The Wind rustled Calliope's curls.

Twelve years to suffer
Twelve years of hate
The Demon's Mark will seal our fate

Calliope grabbed Prewitt's hand. They both recognized the words of the prophecy.

Behind the metallic tune something rose, a sound of tormented weeping. A child's guttural cry of despair, so mournful that it stole tears from Calliope's eyes.

You were not the only child locked away in the dark. There was another. She's still there, a secret prisoner of the mountains— the one with the Demon's Mark.

Calliope sat up straight, wiping her cheeks. "Who? Who is she?"

But the air was suddenly still and silent.

The Wind had vanished, leaving them to face whatever lay around the next bend.

12

Now that the Wind had gone, the world around them crashed into vivid focus.

"There's another girl," said Calliope, pushing herself to her feet. "A girl like me. Did you hear her crying?"

Prewitt nodded.

"We have to save her! We have to set her free."

"We can't get distracted," said Prewitt. "We have the first token, but we still need to find the other two."

Calliope opened her fist. The token shone in her palm, and she knew he was right, but it didn't make her feel better. She shoved the token down onto her finger like a ring. "Afterward, then. No matter what. When this is all over, we'll go and find her and set her free."

"All right," agreed Prewitt.

Calliope let out her breath and looked around, finally allowing herself to take in the world.

The Wind had gone, leaving them with even more questions, but nonetheless, they had solved the first of her mother's clues. They were one step closer to calling the Firebird back. That thrill mingled with the excitement of finally being in open air, rising within her until a wild, untethered bubble of laugher spilled from her lips.

She laughed and laughed and spun around the deck, her soaked shirt slapping against her legs. It was all so new, so intoxicating—the smell of the rain, the feel of it on her skin.

She held out her palms, trying to capture each raindrop as it fell.

She beamed at Prewitt. "Isn't it the most amazing thing you've ever seen?"

He regarded the rain. He was sick to death of it. But as he watched her, spinning, laughing, and squealing around the deck, he couldn't help but laugh, too. She was brave, and unexpected, and somehow, in the midst of all the fear and darkness, she was finding a way to create a bright spot of her own.

"Just listen to it, Prewitt!" Calliope stopped to catch her breath, beaming so wide, her cheeks ached.

The raindrops clinked against the remaining glass windows and struck the metal lanterns. They thudded against the planks and drummed along the top of the carriage, the river a rumble beneath it all.

She went on, dancing and sliding across the deck like a drunken sailor. A dense fog was gathering over the river and pooling along the deck, making it look like Calliope was floating.

Lightning flashed, illuminating the bank, and she ran to

the railing. The misty forms of fog-draped trees framed the sky, and from a distance, she saw the growing outlines of several stout buildings.

Prewitt stood beside her. "The first river city," he said. "It must be!"

In spite of the thickening fog, they could see that the buildings were in poor shape. They were barely standing, and a few had collapsed entirely.

A small figure hunched beside a dilapidated dock, watching them through hollow eyes. A boy, no more than five, stood holding a soaked blanket tight around his shoulders. Prewitt wondered why he was alone, and he scanned the derelict buildings for signs of anyone else. Where were the boy's parents?

"Hello!" Calliope cried, waving at the child. "Hello!"

The blanket dropped from the boy's shoulders, and Calliope sucked in her breath. His bones jutted out, and his collarbone strained against his sallow skin. He lifted a hand, waving shyly back, and as they passed, he ran along the bank, through the thick mud, trying to keep up.

Prewitt felt suddenly guilty. How often had he complained about having to eat fish day in and day out? At least he'd never been truly hungry.

"This is because of the Spectress," hissed Calliope, gripping the gunwale with white-knuckled fingers. "She did this."

A woman darted from behind one of the buildings, and the boy stopped, looking back at her. She motioned frantically at him to return, her eyes flicking to the buildings just ahead of the Barge.

Prewitt's skin prickled, and he followed her gaze, straining to see through the fog. "Cal, I think you should go inside."

"I don't want to go inside. That boy is starving. Can't you see? We have to do something!"

Bells jangled overhead, and Prewitt looked up, scanning the gloom, a feeling of dread weighing him down.

The black shadow of a bird suddenly stamped the clouds.

"Smith's falcons! They found us!" shouted Prewitt. "You have to hide!"

Calliope turned toward the carriage, but it was too late.

Marauders swarmed from behind the buildings, stretching across the riverbank.

For a moment, Prewitt comforted himself with the knowledge that ash golems could not enter the river. Even if the marauders struck their flinty armor, sending sparks blossoming into monsters, the golems would have no place to go. They would be safe as long as they stayed on the Barge, but then he noticed something new.

The marauders had quivers slung across their backs.

A dozen flint-tipped arrows struck steel gloves in perfect unison. Elbows drew back and bowstrings released with eerie grace.

The children could only watch as the arrows arced toward them and ash golems formed in midair. They flew into the fog, maws open, trailing smoke and sparks behind them like monstrous comets. For a moment, they vanished, nothing but a glow within a white wave.

Prewitt and Calliope ran aft toward the poop deck, and the

Barge gave a great, tilting shudder as the first ash golem landed somewhere near the bow.

Prewitt and Calliope crouched, praying that the fog would be enough to hide them.

They felt the golems' collisions one by one and smelled the smoke on the air.

Beside them, the fog bell chimed lightly with each impact, and Prewitt flinched, afraid that it would draw the monsters' attention. He reached up, grabbing hold of the rope, trying to keep the clapper steady on the yawing Barge.

The star glittered. So did his buttons.

"Cal! What was the thing it said in my book again? About the star?" He wished his memory were better.

Calliope spoke without thinking. *"Our patron star shall guide us home, if hope can call it with a tone."*

They glanced at each other. Neither one wanted to go back to the Royal City, but what choice did they have?

"If we ring the bell, the ash golems will know where we're hiding," said Prewitt.

"It's our only chance—unless you want to swim."

The river crashed up against the hull as if daring them to test it.

Prewitt's pulse quickened. It was probably the most reckless thing they could do, and it would likely get them killed sooner rather than later, but they had to try.

He reached up, and with all his might, he rang the bell.

13

The bell called through the fog, and the ash golems turned toward the sound, their molten veins flickering like gathering lightning in a white cloud.

"It's not working," said Prewitt, panic welling in his throat.

The ash golems would soon emerge around the side of the carriage, and there would be no place for them to go except overboard, where they would be slurped down and ground to pieces against the river's rocky spine.

A sudden billow of heat sent the fog spiraling as the carriage went up in flames.

Calliope gasped, pushing away from the railing. "My animals!"

"It's too late!" said Prewitt.

Calliope ran toward the blaze, but before she could reach the door, there was a jolt, as if the Barge had hit a new current, and they staggered back into the railing. The golems were thrown backward, too, and the bell rang louder and louder, rhythmic *bawng*s crashing into one another until they melded into one.

The air vibrated with the sound; even the raindrops trembled as they fell, and then they stopped falling altogether.

The raging river could no longer be heard, and suddenly, a red-orange glow shone through the fog, illuminating the star on the bell, which shimmered and then fell silent.

For a moment, the mist swirled around them, and then everything was still. The Barge no longer moved, and the oars rested in their locks.

At first, Prewitt was certain that the light shining in the gloom must be the Royal City lantern. "We're home," he said, hardly daring to believe it. The patron star had helped them after all. He pushed to the railing.

But where the cliffside should have been, there was nothing. He could see no masts, could hear no roar of the sea. Come to think of it, the air even smelled odd, not the briny, fetid scent of the harbor but something entirely different. It smelled . . . He frowned. What did it smell like? Like the flowers they had found in the Queen's bedroom, the ones with the bobbing heads.

He squinted, trying to understand.

"Cal, I don't think the star took us home at all," he said, turning over his shoulder, but Calliope wasn't there.

He saw her slip into the carriage just as the door collapsed in the flames, just as the golems turned their eyeless faces toward the carriage windows, pulling fog into their nostrils and preparing their furnaces for a final conflagration.

Prewitt couldn't move, couldn't think.

But suddenly, there was a loud *crack*, and two of the golems' heads were ripped away in a violent spray of lava and ash. More *crack*s followed, sending sparking bodies scattering across the deck.

Prewitt didn't hesitate. He ran for the door. He ducked inside and found Calliope, surrounded by shrinking stacks of burning books. She reached toward the window seat, flinching as she swept charred flakes off the melting velvet and into her palm. "They're gone," she said. "Brown Bear, Hippo, Lion. They're all gone."

"We don't have time for that now," hissed Prewitt, pulling her down to a crouch. He peered up over the ledge. "Something is happening. Someone is here."

Ghostly figures were materializing all across the Barge, flying over the gunwales in a salvo of *crack*s, swaths of white fabric streaming behind them through the mist.

They moved swiftly and silently as they faded in and out of the murk, and it was impossible to tell how many of them there were or if they were even human.

"What are they?" asked Calliope. "Are they spirits?"

Prewitt shook his head. "I don't know."

He had never seen anyone fight an ash golem, and even though it was happening right in front of him, he couldn't quite believe it. The figures swirled and struck in perfect unison. Sharp *crack*s staccatoed the foggy silence as they flung out long green ropes and tore limbs from monstrous bodies without hesitation.

He fully expected the ash golems to rise stronger than ever, but before they could, the figures hurled small, round objects that burst in showers of water, dousing the sparks. The monsters released final breaths of sizzling steam and were gone for good.

It was over in moments, the ash golems nothing but wet heaps, and the mysterious figures had gathered in a clutch on the row deck, white smudges behind a veil of fog.

"Come out," someone ordered. "We know you are in there."

Prewitt glanced at Calliope. "You have to hide! They can't find you here!"

Calliope's eyes were red. "But they saved us. They might be friends. We're home, aren't we?"

Prewitt shook his head. "This isn't the Royal City, Cal. I don't know who these people are—or if they're even people. We don't know if we can trust them."

"What about you?" she asked. "Shouldn't you hide, too?"

"It'll be okay. I'm a boy. But if they see you, they'll know right away that something is going on."

Calliope hesitated, then opened her mouth to argue.

"I'm the other half of the moon," said Prewitt. "You have to let me do my part."

Calliope nodded once and wiped the ash from her paper animals onto her pants. She turned and fled to her cabin.

Prewitt took a deep breath, trying to steady his nerves. He tugged down the bottom of his jacket and pushed through the door to the quarterdeck. All at once, the fog rolled back like a curtain, and Prewitt couldn't keep the shock from tugging his mouth open.

The sky above was a fading blue, and what he'd thought was the city lantern must be the *sun*. It was sinking warm and orange toward the horizon, dragging the sky from blue, to periwinkle, to pink, and then to red.

He stood, astonished, trying to make sense of what he was seeing, but before he could, a *crack* sent a whip biting into his wrist. He cried out and tried to wrench himself free. The whip was a strange, bright green, and the more he tried to pull away, the more it tightened, until his fingers began to swell and turn purple.

He howled as he was dragged down the steps, but the person on the other side of the whip showed no mercy, and his boots dragged across the sparkling black sand from Calliope's broken hourglass. He tripped along the wreckage of the row deck and fell to his knees. When he looked up, he finally saw the faces of the ghostly figures who had destroyed the golems.

Before him stood eight girls in identical white dresses, wearing eight identical stony expressions. For a moment, Prewitt couldn't believe what he was seeing. How was it possible? The girls all had to be around eleven or twelve years old.

He felt the blood drain from his face. They were working

for the Spectress! How else could they have learned to fight ash golems that way?

One of the girls stepped forward. She flicked her wrist, and Prewitt was yanked to his feet. The girl reeled him close, looping the green lash round and round until they stood within a nose length.

She glared down at him with odd eyes—one brown, one gray—and her voice was cool and even as she said, "Tell me who you are and why you brought monsters to the Halcyon Glade."

14

The Bookkeeper had just pulled the heavy curtain aside to lead the Bargemaster out into the shop's atrium when he heard glass shatter.

A moment later, pulling sand and crystal from his pocket, Meredith's composure shattered, too. "Calliope!" he shouted, and the shards had slipped from his fingers as he hurled himself down into the tunnels and thundered back toward the Cavern, but he didn't get far before he was met by sweltering ash golems, devouring ancient books draught by draught into unrepentant bellies.

He turned, running back the way he'd come, but the smoke quickly overtook him, and he crumpled to the stone floor, his vision blurring to darkness.

When at last he opened his eyes, the tunnels were gone, and he found himself back in the Bookkeeper's tiny room in the Firebird Tale and Tome.

The Bookkeeper sat on a wooden chair beside the bed, pouring black sand between his palms. "The twin glasses," he said. "The first gifts from the Nymph Isles. Sent with two unusual storm glasses, if my memory serves me. But how could the second hourglass have broken unless someone was on the Barge to break it?" His voice was smooth. "After all, that's where the second glass has always been kept, and I know you like your conventions."

Meredith ignored him, jumping to his feet. The room reeled its complaint as he bent and reached for the hatch. Before his mind could register the Bookkeeper's warning, he scorched his palm on the searing metal. He staggered back. The fire was still raging through the tunnels. It raged through his mind, too, fear and hopelessness burning away everything calm and ordered, and it was a moment before he realized that the Bookkeeper was still speaking.

"When you didn't return, I knew something must have happened. I went searching for answers. It was a miracle I found you in time. You were in shock, barely conscious, but somehow I got you standing. We managed to make it here just ahead of the blaze." His glasses misted. "My books made for excellent kindling."

"I don't care about your books!" snapped Meredith, wheeling on him. "I have to get back to the Cavern!" He strode across the floor, yanking aside the curtain and sweeping into the atrium, careful to stay out of the flickering lantern light.

The Bookkeeper scurried after him, slippers splashing

through the rainwater that pooled across the parquet floor. "Where do you intend to go? You can't leave."

"I'll go to the castle. I may still be able to get in through the nursery." It was Meredith's only hope. He reached the shop door, his fingers grasping the handle, and with a jolt, he understood what the Bookkeeper was trying to say.

Waves beat against the half-moon window, and seaweed sludge mocked in a lurid slide behind the boards. While he had slept, the tide had come in. He was trapped.

He swore, pulling his cap from his head. "I have to find a way back!" he said. "I have to get to the Cavern before . . . before . . ."

"Before the Spectress finds the Princess?"

Meredith blinked. "You knew. All this time? Why didn't you say anything?"

"Of course I knew. The moment you started asking for books about history and legends and tales of Lyrica, I knew. Those stories have never been your taste. Why didn't you ask for my guidance? I know many things that could have been helpful to her. If you'd confided in me, I'd gladly have gone and tutored her in all the things a Princess should know. My knowledge is varied and passed down through generations. It would have been far more helpful to her than the limited knowledge of a Bargemaster."

"The Queen made me promise to keep the girl a secret. To keep her safe."

"She couldn't have meant from me," said the Bookkeeper.

Meredith changed the subject. "The golems may not have breached the Cavern. There would be no way for them to get in unless the Princess opened the door."

The Bookkeeper rubbed his head. "There's something you must see." He led the way back to his desk where a pile of glass lay beneath a mounted magnifying glass. He nodded toward it, and the Bargemaster bent close. "The remains of your hourglass," he said.

Meredith staggered back. The shards of the hourglass were coated in soot. "No."

The Bookkeeper nodded. "Yes. You know what this means. The twin hourglass—the Princess's glass—has been touched by golem's breath."

"There has to be another explanation," said Meredith, refusing to believe it. "It's—it's only my hourglass that's been touched. I—I must have had it with me in the tunnels."

"Come now," said the Bookkeeper. "We both know that your hourglass, *this hourglass*, broke in your pocket without any cause from you. It's what sent you running back into the tunnels. It broke because its twin broke. The only way the glass could be soot-covered is if something happened to its twin. The golems have most certainly found the girl—or at the very least, her hourglass. Whether or not she still lives, well . . ." He trailed off, his hands out to the side, one palm still full of black sand.

Meredith crumpled his cap between his palms. He had refused to let Calliope come with him, had told her it was too dangerous. But danger had come to her anyway.

He shoved the cap back onto his head. "I have to know for sure."

Jack sat on the city steps a long time after Prewitt had disappeared into the Bookshop. The Bargeboy's words wound round and round in his head until his brain was bound in knots.

I thought you would want to help! After what they did to your parents! Don't you even care?

He did care. Of course he did. But he couldn't fight the Spectress. His parents had defied her, and look what had happened to them.

Still, it gnawed at him, a relentless gnat of a thought: What if Prewitt was right, and the Princess really was alive?

His fingers plucked at the nets.

He imagined how life could change if the Princess sang the Song and the Firebird returned, but dreaming made his stomach ache. What right did he have to think about how things *could* be? Things were the way they were, and he should be grateful because at least he was alive.

He worked in a trance, his fingers laboring of their own accord beneath the chatter of his thoughts.

The tide came in, and the boats went out, and he remained until something made him look up. Someone had torn away the slats from one of the windows in the Bookshop, and a person was waving furiously at him.

Jack frowned, squinting through the rain.

"Jack!" The nets fell from Jack's fingers. It was the

Bargemaster. Another figure appeared behind him, bent and ancient, and Jack realized that it must be the Bookkeeper.

"Jack!" the Bargemaster shouted again. "Go and bring a dory! There's one tied up at the edge of the second tier."

Jack hesitated, looking down at the turbulent water. Waves crashed furiously against the bottom stories of the shop as if determined to tow it under layer by layer.

The Bargemaster shouted again. "You can do it, Jack!"

Jack shook his head. "I can't—not by myself!"

The Bargemaster turned his head, speaking with the Bookkeeper. Finally, he turned back. "It's all right. Go and get Cedric and Old Harry! Tell them it's urgent."

Jack didn't need to be told again. He ran across the tiers, and in a few minutes, he was back, the two watermen in tow. He had found them cleaning fish behind the abandoned butcher shop, and before he had finished telling them what he'd seen, they had flung down their gutting knives and raced across the tier.

A crashing wave swept through the open window and sloshed down the steps as the dory bumped up against the Bookshop wall.

"What's going on?" asked Cedric.

The Bargemaster climbed into the boat. "Ash golems," he said. "They've broken into the tunnels. I've got to find a way past them to the Sacred Cavern."

Cedric swore. "Ash golems? What are they doing down there?"

"A better question would be, what were *you* doing down there, Meredith?" asked Old Harry. "And why do you need to get to the Cavern?"

Jack peered through the window, past the old man, who seemed to be struggling with whether or not to join them. Water gushed through the window and spilled down the steps.

"Where's Prewitt?" Jack asked.

The Bargemaster's head whipped around. "Prewitt? What do you mean?"

"I saw him go inside," said Jack. "But he didn't come out again."

The color drained from the Bargemaster's face as he swung toward the Bookkeeper. "You didn't tell me."

The Bookkeeper's watery eyes met Meredith's, but there was no apology in them. "The boy came looking for answers. He deserved to know the truth."

The Bargemaster pulled at his mustache. "*What did you do?* Tell me you didn't send him to find her, Thomas. Tell me you aren't the reason that the ash golems got into the tunnels."

The Bookkeeper stepped into the boat, wobbling as he sat down, his knees pushed up to his ears and his bathrobe flapping. "When someone comes looking for information, I have a duty as the Bookkeeper to provide—"

"Duty! Don't tell *me* about duty! No, for you it's all about the story."

The Bookkeeper wiped fog from his glasses. "Judge me all you like, but would you keep the boy from his *destiny*? The

Princess is the Age of Hope, Bargemaster. You know as well as anyone that the time for action is now."

"Destiny! What are you talking about, Thomas?"

"Why, the two halves of the moon, of course. The Princess and the Bargeboy."

Meredith's face flushed scarlet, and a bead of sweat trembled in his eyebrow. "Are you telling me that you sent my son into danger, that you risked your Princess's life, because of a prophecy you claim to have found at the Nymph Isles?"

"A prophecy that could save—"

Meredith exploded. "How could you be so foolish? Even if you could trust this prophecy, you have no idea if you're interpreting it correctly. You could have sent my son and the Princess to their deaths—or is that the *destiny* of which you speak so reverently?"

The Bookkeeper bristled. "The Ancient Spirits wish us no harm. They only left to keep themselves safe, and who can blame them for that? They respected my search for knowledge and wisdom and my willingness to sacrifice for their attainment. This is why they rewarded me with a gift of their prescience."

Cedric's and Old Harry's glances caught, but it was Jack who spoke up.

"The Princess is alive? But that means Prewitt was right! He knew it all along!"

Neither the Bookkeeper nor the Bargemaster answered. The air was tense as they stared each other down. Lightning fractured the sky and flashed across their furious faces.

Old Harry rowed through the tension, and soon the little boat rammed against the stone retaining wall on the edge of the second tier. Cedric tossed Jack the rope, and Jack quickly tied the dory to the mooring ring. The nerves in his fingers hummed with the news that the Princess really was alive. But Jack realized that it also meant he had lost his opportunity. Prewitt had asked him to come along, had asked for help, but he had been too afraid, too uncertain.

He crawled up onto the tier, and the watermen followed, but the Bargemaster and the Bookkeeper remained in the boat, waging a silent war in the hull.

Old Harry cleared his throat, pulling off his cap and running his hand through a puff of white hair. "Would one of you kindly explain what is going on? The tiers are strangely empty at the moment. Not a marauder in sight. I wonder if it has anything to do with whatever you're not telling us."

The other men looked up toward the tents. Old Harry was right; the marauders had vanished.

Meredith sighed. "I suppose it's time you knew."

He and the Bookkeeper climbed up onto the tier, and the watermen and Jack stood together in the rain while the Bargemaster finally told them everything.

"So she really did survive," said Old Harry, shaking his head. "And here we were believing you when you told us you couldn't remember what had happened after the Terrible Thing. We thought all the trauma had damaged part of your brain."

"Now you understand why I have to get to the Sacred

Cavern, but the tunnels are on fire and there's enough kindling down there to keep the golems fed for a long time."

"My poor books," moaned the Bookkeeper.

The Bargemaster's fists clenched. "Your books? What about my son?"

"All right, all right, let's all just calm down," said Old Harry, placing a hand on Meredith's shoulder. "We have no reason to suspect that the children have been harmed. They may be safe and sound inside the Cavern. You know it's impenetrable."

Meredith shook his head. He told the watermen about the soot-stained glass.

"Can I see?" asked Jack.

"We left it back in the shop, but here," said the Bookkeeper. He held out his hand, pouring the black sand he'd been holding into Jack's open palms.

The men started discussing options, and soon they were arguing.

Jack squatted down, peering at the sand. He'd never seen sand so black. He let it sift between his fingers, and as it did, it began to change, as if by magic. It glittered, sparkling and shimmering until it was almost blinding.

"Look!" said Jack. The men went on arguing, and he shouted again. "Look!"

They turned toward him. None of them had ever heard Jack shout before, but the normally timid boy seemed different, taller than he'd been that morning.

"What is it, Jack?" asked Old Harry. "What's going on?"

"Something is happening to the sand!"

"Let me see." The Bookkeeper reached into his bathrobe pocket and pulled out a loop, clipping it to his glasses. He bent over Jack's palm.

The Bookkeeper's brows met. "It's almost as if . . ." He shook his head.

"What?" The Bargemaster looked like he was about to unravel.

"It's as if the sand from the twin hourglass, wherever it is, is somehow in direct sunlight."

"That's impossible," said Cedric. "The sun hasn't shone in Lyrica in twelve years."

"No," said the Bookkeeper. "The sun has not shone on the realm of *mankind*."

Meredith stood up straighter. "The Halcyon Glade," he whispered. "Is it possible? But how could they have gotten there? No human has stepped foot inside the Glade for hundreds of years."

Old Harry rubbed his chin. "My mother told me tales of the Glade, where spirits dwelled and animals could talk. She said humans could never go there unless a spirit gave them entrance."

Jack felt a thrill warm his chest. "Maybe a spirit *did* give them entrance," he said.

The Bargemaster pulled his cap down onto his head. "We have to go and find them."

"Hold on, now," said Old Harry. "We don't know for sure they're in the Halcyon Glade. It's only a guess."

"A guess based on an ancient fairy tale." Cedric scoffed. "Spirits, and beasts, ancient trees, and redheaded giants. You can't seriously believe that we're going to go and find it all. It's nothing but a children's story."

The Bookkeeper sputtered, but Meredith interrupted. "A guess is all we have. It's something."

"It's hope," said Jack.

The Bargemaster looked at him. "Yes, and we are not going to let it go to waste."

The knots in Jack's head unsnarled. He was getting his second chance. "Can I come?"

Meredith looked at him. "It'll be dangerous."

"Please," said Jack. "I'm not afraid."

Meredith flinched. That's what Prewitt had said before he'd made him swear not to go looking for the Princess. He wished—but what good was wishing? There was no sense in it. "You can come if Old Harry says it's all right."

Jack looked up at Old Harry, who shrugged. "What's a little more danger these days?"

The Bookkeeper held up a finger. "There's just one more thing," he said.

"What?" snapped Meredith.

"We mustn't forget who governs the Halcyon Glade," said the Bookkeeper. "If the children have found themselves there, it is very unlikely that her reception has been a welcoming one."

The men looked at each other. The words seemed to hold meaning for everyone but Jack.

"Who?" he asked.

The Bookkeeper wiped the rain from his glasses with the sleeve of his robe. "The one who hid the Halcyon Glade in the first place: the Wild Woman. She hates humans—perhaps more than any of the other spirits. The children will get no kindness from her."

"Then there's no time to lose," said Meredith. "We have to get there as soon as possible."

"Now, let's all wait a minute," said Old Harry. "We're talking about the Halcyon Glade here. We aren't going to just wander into it. Every story I've ever heard says it's hidden."

"Hidden from the eyes of *humankind*," said Meredith pointedly.

"Ah," said the Bookkeeper, brightening. "Clever."

The two men nodded at each other, their quarrel momentarily forgotten.

"Yes, exactly," said Old Harry. "That's what I just said. It's *hidden*." He gave Cedric a look. Maybe trauma *had* damaged the Bargemaster's brain after all.

Meredith ran a finger along his mustache. "It's time we paid the Falconer a visit."

15

The paper animals burned in Calliope's mind as she hid inside the window seat.

She hadn't been able to protect them. They had been her friends, had depended on her to keep them safe, and now they were gone.

If you really look, you'll see that you're still just a girl, no older or wiser than you were yesterday.

Except she was older. She was so much older. Far, far older than twelve. She had lived a thousand years in the span of a single day.

There was a click beyond the darkness. Someone had opened the cabin door.

Calliope tensed. She lay, not daring to breathe, as gentle footsteps padded across her room. She heard her wardrobe door open and shut, then the sound of footsteps going back up the stairs.

She waited for what felt like hours, her legs cramping and

her imagination going wild. She told herself to be patient, that Prewitt would come, but finally, she knew she couldn't bear it any longer. She had to know what was happening.

She pressed up the lid of the window seat, peeking out.

The room was empty, but the light was different, strange and golden. She unfolded herself, stretching as she turned toward the window.

She clapped her hand across her mouth. What she saw was so astounding that she stood frozen for a long time, trying to make her eyes believe it.

The sky beyond was a hazy purple, and sunshine streamed in red-gold beams. The river had vanished, and in its place was rolling grass, lush and green and dotted with daisies.

Calliope pushed open the door of her cabin and stepped out into the carriage.

"Prewitt?" she whispered, but there was no answer.

The Barge was a mess. Everything was charred, and Calliope realized just how close they'd come to being killed.

The two storm glasses on the table were soot-stained but intact. She reached out her arm and brushed one with her sleeve. Beneath the grime, the crystals promised sun.

Sun. Calliope looked up, taking in the drowsy beams stretching through the window, shaped by dust and ash.

Could this be the Halcyon Glade? Her skin pricked. She had always wanted to know more about the Glade, but hardly any of her books had mentioned it beyond the legend of its birth. Was that because no one had ever seen it? Or because no one had survived long enough to write anything down?

She tugged her curls. She needed to find Prewitt.

She tiptoed out onto the abandoned deck. He was nowhere in sight, and the strange, ghostly figures were gone.

Calliope swallowed, looking around at the wreckage.

Her home was in ruins. Her animals were gone. But she still had one friend left, and she was determined to find out what had happened to him.

She climbed overboard, her bare feet landing in the cool, damp grass. She tossed her curls, refusing to let herself enjoy it.

As she stomped through streams of sparkling water burbling between knolls and huffed along daisy paths that led over soft hillocks, she began to get a strange feeling. It started in her toes and tingled up to the base of her neck. She stopped a moment to look at the beautiful fruit trees draping their branches across the streams.

At first glance, it was all idyllic, nature at its loveliest, thriving and sure. The scent of pollen hung in the early-evening air, and bumblebees buzzed in the gently rustling leaves. But beneath the beauty, Calliope sensed that something was not quite right.

When she stepped close to the tree, she saw that there were black splotches on the leaves like ink dripped onto parchment. *The Demon's Mark will seal our fate.*

She frowned. Why had that phrase popped into her head? Calliope wrapped her arms around herself. Everything was not as it seemed here, but she couldn't let herself get distracted. She had to find Prewitt.

She had walked only a few minutes more when she reached a village. Cottages sprouted straight out of the ground, formed entirely from living plants, branches winding up to form roofs thick with foliage.

She looked around for someone who might be able to answer her questions, but the entire place seemed abandoned.

A raven followed her, hopping along arched gables, winging gently among the cottages.

"Where is everyone?" she demanded, but the bird only blinked.

Calliope came to a cottage that was larger than the others and almost perfectly round. A porch wrapped the outside, and sleepy sunshine played with vines that wound up around tree-trunk pillars and across twisting branches that formed the gable.

The door stood wide open, a wreath of red berries hanging across it. Calliope climbed the porch and peered inside. "Hello? Is anyone here?"

When no one answered, she stepped cautiously over the threshold, looking for any sign of Prewitt. The rotting fruit, the abandoned village, and the silent cottage made acid churn in Calliope's stomach. Something was not right here, and the longer she spent searching without any sign of him, the more concerned she became.

Soft light twinkled down through woven birch boughs, and delicate moss carpeted the floor. Twigs and branches twisted around the circular walls, forming shelves that held shining feathers, small jars filled with bright liquids, and sparkling stones of assorted sizes.

Small beds were positioned around the wall in various states, some made neatly, others a heap of quilts. At the end of each bed sat a wooden chest.

There were names carved into each chest in careful, looping letters. She bent to get a closer look and nearly stumbled over a woven basket on the floor near the bedpost. Water sloshed over the side, seeping down into the moss.

Calliope peered into the basket. There was *something* coiled inside, something that looked very much like a green snake, waiting to jump up and snap at her fingers.

She gulped and looked around, realizing that there were baskets of water positioned by each bed.

She moved back to the chest, watching her step more carefully, and ran her fingers across the name *Fi*. She reached down to the wooden clasp, unlatching it and pushing open the heavy lid. For a moment, she wasn't quite sure what she was seeing.

She sat back on her haunches, bewildered. The chest was full of clothing, dresses all in white gossamer with lace around the hems. She reached in, carefully gathering the fabric into her arms. It smelled like pine. Underneath, at the very bottom of the chest, lay a single colored item.

Calliope sucked in her breath, setting aside the dress, and gently pulled out a tiny infant's garment. It was light blue with delicate red flowers crocheted at the waist. She was about to replace it when she noticed a piece of parchment tucked carefully into the collar. It had been folded and refolded, and there were marks where the ink had run.

Wild Woman, great Spirit of the Halcyon Glade, mistress over all things that grow in the sunlight, we beg you take mercy on our baby girl. Keep her safe in these wicked times, and return her to us if ever the world is set right.

Her name is Fi

Calliope's mind reeled. Meredith had said that girls had been taken from their parents' arms in search of her. Had some been saved?

She read the parchment again. *Wild Woman.* She thought of the words on the wall. *Wind, Woman, Thief.*

Could this be the *Woman*? Could *she* have the second token?

Her pulse prodded her on, faster and faster, as she moved from chest to chest. There were eight in all: Fi, Poppy, Giana, Maddie, Becca, Hazel, Lanna, and finally Ilsbeth.

Every one held a similar piece of parchment, each addressed to the Wild Woman, each sounding desperate and hopeless. When Calliope got to the bed nearest the door and the trunk marked Ilsbeth, she dug around, searching, but there was no letter.

She pulled everything out of the chest and was shaking out

the baby garment a second time when something green and stinging lashed her wrist.

"Get away from my trunk, intruder!"

Calliope yelped, trying to pull away, but she was jerked around, her elbow cracking. She tried to wrench herself free, but the more she pulled, the more the lash bit into her skin, clenching her tighter and tighter as she struggled.

"You're hurting me!" She tripped across the moss as she was yanked toward the figure silhouetted in the doorway. A stream of golden light shifted through the boughs, and a face was suddenly illuminated.

Calliope's eyes widened. So this was Ilsbeth.

It was a girl, not much older than Calliope but several heads taller. Her bare arms rippled with muscle. Her hair was black and slick as ink, pulled starkly away from her face, which was inscrutable, lips pressed tightly together, high, bronzed brow clear. Only her eyes gave her away, one a dark, melting brown, the other a chilling gray. They darted back and forth, taking Calliope in. "You were aboard the *Queen's Barge*," she accused. "Your friend told us he was alone, but we knew he was lying."

"Where is he?" Calliope demanded, trying not to let her nerves show. "You'd better not have hurt him!"

Ilsbeth tilted her head. "You would not speak to me that way if you understood the severity of what you have done. Either you are stupid and do not know where you are or you do not realize the consequences of trespassing here."

"I know where I am," snapped Calliope. "This is the

Halcyon Glade. But we weren't *trying* to trespass; we were *brought* here. The patron star—"

Ilsbeth lifted her palm. "I do not care how you came to be here. Tell me who you are. Tell me how a scrawny girl with no fighting ability has managed to stay alive in the world beyond the Glade."

Calliope was offended. She stood up straighter. "I am the Princess of Lyrica!"

Even as the truth fell from her lips, she could hear Prewitt's exaggerated sigh, could imagine him telling her she should be more careful, but she pressed his voice away. She needed to find out what had happened to him. She needed the girl's trust, and the fastest way to earn it was by telling the truth.

She told Ilsbeth everything. She told her about growing up in the Cavern and about her decision to leave. She told her about meeting Prewitt, about the words on the wall, and about their escape through the tunnels. She told her about calling the Wind and about the token it had given her.

Ilsbeth's hand flicked, and the green lash dropped from Calliope's wrist, the skin beneath furious and swollen. "You summoned an Ancient Spirit?"

Calliope nodded.

"It came? It helped you?" Ilsbeth looked utterly bewildered by the idea.

"We had to give it our secrets, and we had to take one in return." Calliope shuddered, remembering the sound of the crying girl, of the tinkling song.

"But why did you trust this boy? Why did you let him follow you on this quest?"

"He's not following me. He's helping. He's my friend."

Ilsbeth hissed through her teeth. "How can he be your friend? He can never understand you. He will never know what it is to have to hide because just being yourself is dangerous."

"That's not his fault," said Calliope. "It hasn't been easy for him, either, you know. It's bad for everyone. That's why we have to set things right again. It's why we have to call the Firebird back."

Ilsbeth pressed her lips together. She shifted from foot to foot, her eyes unblinking; then she let out her breath all at once. "Fine. If you are really determined to save him, then we should go."

"Save him? Save him from what? What did you do to him?" Calliope peppered Ilsbeth with questions as she chased her across the knolls.

"The only reason we even allowed the boy to live in the first place is because of the mysterious way that boat appeared, but he let monsters into our Glade, and he had to answer for it. We took him to the Guardians for questioning."

"You mean you would have *killed* him? But you're just a girl! How could you think of hurting anyone?"

Ilsbeth stopped suddenly, pivoting to glare at Calliope. "*Just a girl*? What do you mean by that? Tell me, where are the rest of the girls in this world?"

Her gaze was so intense that Calliope couldn't bring herself to answer.

Ilsbeth nodded. "That's right. The Spectress didn't care, did she? No. So don't you ever say that you're *just a girl* again. If you truly think that, then you've already lost, and I'm wasting my time helping you."

She broke away into a run without waiting for an answer, her white dress sweeping out behind her, painted pink in the fading light.

Calliope thought about that as she ran after Ilsbeth. She had always felt chided by Meredith's words. They had been meant to make her understand how small she was, how helpless. To remind her that she had a responsibility to stay where she was safe while older, wiser people protected her.

But Ilsbeth and the others were girls, just like her, and that hadn't made them small or weak; it hadn't made them hide away in a cavern while other people fought their battles. She had seen them destroy ash golems without any fear, and they had done it all on their own.

Ilsbeth slowed just as the sun sank beneath the horizon. They had reached two long rows of elms, their branches tangled in a tight embrace. Between the rows sat a long, curved bench, which, like everything else, seemed to grow out of the ground.

A pair of girls in white dresses waited on the bench, their legs dangling. They were opposites in nearly every way. One tall, the other slight; one dark, one fair. The taller girl stood when she saw them, her eyes questioning.

"This is the Princess of Lyrica, Calliope," said Ilsbeth before the girl could ask. "She is looking for the boy, but I see we are too late."

"*Too late*? What do you mean?" Calliope's voice squeaked, panic tightening her throat.

The taller girl cast a quick glance at Calliope, but the other stared straight ahead, green eyes clear and unseeing. Her hair was braided and hung over her shoulders like two slim sheaves of wheat. It was this girl who spoke, her voice soothing and her words unhurried.

"Welcome, Princess of Lyrica. I am Fi, and this is Hazel. The Guardians questioned your friend. They asked who he was and why he had come. They wanted to know how he had managed to pilot the *Queen's Barge* without assistance and what spirit had brought him here."

"What did he say?" asked Calliope.

"He refused to answer their questions," snapped Hazel, looking Calliope up and down. "He was quite stubborn."

Fi nodded. "Even when they threatened him, he did not give in. He did not tell them anything about you, Princess, although it might have saved him."

Calliope felt the blood drain from her cheeks. "You don't mean— They haven't—"

"They threatened to take him to the Wild Woman. They told him that she does not take pity on strangers—especially strange boys. But he did not react the way they expected."

"What do you mean?"

"He whooped," said Hazel dryly, "and then he refused to cooperate at all."

Ilsbeth frowned. "Why would he—"

"I know why," groaned Calliope, pressing her hand to her forehead. Of course, as soon as they had mentioned the Wild Woman, Prewitt must have suspected exactly what she had. "You have to take me to him!"

Three heads turned toward her. "You cannot be serious," said Ilsbeth. "Did you not hear what Fi just said? The Wild Woman does not like strangers. She barely tolerates us."

"Please!" said Calliope, practically jumping up and down. "Don't you see? It's my fault! I'm the reason he wants to see her. I can't be the reason he gets hurt."

Fi's eyes drifted upward. "This boy risks his life for you."

"Not just for me. For the kingdom—for you! He thinks the Wild Woman can help us all. That she can help us call the Firebird back to Lyrica."

"The words the Queen left on the wall," said Ilsbeth, remembering what Calliope had told her. "Wind. Woman. Thief. You think the Wild Woman is the woman from your mother's clue?"

Calliope nodded. "Yes! Don't you see? We have to go now! If it's true, if she is the woman, then she will help, but only if she knows that I am here, and Prewitt will never give me away!"

The girls looked at one another.

Calliope stamped her foot. "We have to hurry! You said yourself that she would kill him as soon as she saw him!"

Ilsbeth was unmoved, and Calliope wanted to grab her by the shoulders and shake her. She needed their help, needed them to care. Only they knew where the Guardians had taken Prewitt.

"Don't you see?" she asked, desperate to make them understand. "If the Wild Woman really is the woman from my mother's clues, then I'm one step closer to calling the Firebird back—one step closer to defeating the Spectress. You won't have to stay in the Glade anymore. You will finally be able to go home to your parents. Isn't that what you want?"

"It is very unlikely that the Wild Woman is the woman you seek," said Ilsbeth. "She would never help the realm of humankind. Not after what they did."

"What do you think, Fi?" Hazel turned to the smaller girl.

Fi tilted her head, thinking for a long moment. Calliope could barely contain her impatience.

Finally, Fi spoke. "Are we sisters?"

"Of course," said Hazel and Ilsbeth together.

"What binds us if not blood?"

"The fight," said Ilsbeth.

"Survival," said Hazel.

"And loss, too?" asked Fi.

"Yes, loss most of all," said Ilsbeth, mouth tight.

"Then the Princess must also be our sister, for she has lost, and fought, and survived just as we have—only she has done it all alone, with only this *boy* to help her."

Ilsbeth and Hazel looked at each other, and finally, Ilsbeth nodded.

"All right, Princess of Lyrica, we will help you."

16

"This is your last chance, boy."

An enormous man glared down at Prewitt, his wild red mane rippling in the low breeze. He was larger than any man Prewitt had ever seen before, and there was a presence about him that was not human at all. There was no forgetting that the Halcyon Glade was a place meant for spirits, and a scrawny human boy who couldn't read and knew nothing about the world did not belong.

"I am Ardal," the man had said when the Glade Girls had deposited Prewitt at his feet between the elms. "The Guardian of the Halcyon Glade, and these are my sons." An orange fox stood on high alert at Ardal's heel, hackles raised.

A row of green eyes had glared down at him. The sons were nearly identical copies of the man, younger but equally hirsute. They wore vests of brown leather, open at the chest, and on their backs hung heavy bronze shields that flashed in the fading light.

The questioning had begun at once. Except the questions didn't *feel* like questions. Every movement, every word exploded with a force of blame without any room for innocence, and Prewitt knew that it didn't matter how he answered. His guilt had already been determined. He had come to a place where humans were not allowed.

"You? How could you pilot the *Queen's Barge* all alone? The truth now, boy, or you will be taken before the Wild Woman and she will determine your fate."

Prewitt had tensed. *The Wild Woman?* The memory of the words on the wall swam before his eyes.

Ardal had nodded. "I see you've heard of her. You're wise to be afraid."

But Prewitt hadn't been afraid. He'd been so elated, he hadn't even realized that he'd let out a whoop until he caught the confusion on Ardal's face.

He and the other Guardians had looked at one another, unnerved by Prewitt's lack of fear, and the questions had continued. But this time, Prewitt hadn't even pretended to cooperate.

He knew what he had to do. He had to find out if the Wild Woman really was the woman from the clues. But he also had to be certain that Cal was safe before anything he said could give her away.

The men had grown more and more frustrated, and finally

their patience was spent. Ardal had dragged him across the knolls toward a glassy pond, threatening with each step, detailing all the ways the Wild Woman would torture and maim him if he did not give in and tell them what they wanted to know.

But now, standing at the edge of the pond, the evening breeze cool off the water, Ardal's manner suddenly changed.

"All right, boy, it is not too late. Even now, we will show mercy. Just tell us the truth." His new tone made Prewitt nervous. It was clear that Ardal had not wanted it to come to this, that he had hoped Prewitt would break before they reached the pond's edge.

Prewitt glanced back over his shoulder.

Even the girls had not been allowed to come near the pond. They were barely visible a long way off in the twilight, a blur of white against the blackening hillocks. He could sense the tension in them. But what could frighten girls who had fought ash golems? Girls who had done what even his own father would not.

Fireflies danced in the willow copse that surrounded the bank, and a frog warned from the reeds: *give up, give up, give up.*

"I am the kind one here," said Ardal. "The Wild Woman will not be merciful. There is nothing you can say that will protect you from her wrath."

Prewitt's heart squeezed, and perhaps it was the way the moon was rising above the horizon, casting long, eerie shadows across the pond, but for the first time, he wondered if he'd miscalculated.

"Just tell us why you were aboard the *Queen's Barge*, the *real* reason this time. Tell us why the ash golems attacked you. Tell us why the Spectress wants you dead."

Ardal's huge hand wrapped around Prewitt's shoulder, and he leaned closer. He smelled of freshly chopped spruce and soft leather. "Tell us and spare yourself."

The Guardians murmured as they watched and waited for Prewitt's answer. Was the child foolish enough to deliver his own death sentence?

Prewitt gulped; he could feel fear rising within him, but he refused to let it control him. If this was the *Woman* the Queen had wanted him to find, then he had a duty to face her, and if she wasn't—well, then at least Prewitt had kept Calliope safe. He would not be a bystander this time.

"I demand an audience with the Wild Woman."

Ardal shook his head. "Foolish child," he said. But Prewitt thought he heard a hint of admiration in his tone.

Ardal stepped to the edge of the pond, fox on his heels, and held out a huge hand. "Wild Woman, I, Ardal, Guardian of the Halcyon Glade, bid you appear."

For a moment, nothing happened. But Ardal remained where he was, and the moon rose ever higher, casting light between his knuckles. Shadows expanded like cell bars across the grass, climbing up Prewitt's ruined pants legs. He shivered.

The air cooled, and the branches of the willows began to swing back and forth in eerie unison, slowly at first, like dancers at a twilight ball, then picking up pace little by little. Faster and faster they swung, until they were a frenzy of limbs, flinging up water and muck from the pond. It spattered the men's cheeks, but they held their positions, hands at their sides.

"Wild Woman, I, Ardal, Guardian of the Halcyon Glade, bid you appear. Appear and judge this stranger who invokes your name!"

The branches were riotous now, grasping and clawing the dirt like skeletal fingers starving for skin. Prewitt wanted to turn and run, but he stayed, frozen and afraid.

She appeared then, melting from the black shadow of a willow trunk across the pond.

Prewitt's mouth dropped open as the woman emerged, stepping her way across the surface of the water, her tread delicate on unwavering lily pads. Her skin glowed in the moonlight, and her hair gleamed pure silver as it cascaded down, trailing through the water behind her. Instead of fabric, she was clothed by willow branches that wound around her slight frame, sweeping in long, soft-leafed layers that fluttered against her bare feet.

But the moment she stepped onto the bank, *she changed.*

It was faster than a blink, one moment a woman, the next a *beast* so hideous and terrible that Prewitt hid his face. Any elation he'd felt at solving the Queen's clue evaporated, and he knew at once that he had made a grave error. He had never felt more human or more inadequate.

His hands shook, and his entire body trembled from deep within, as if his soul had turned to ice. He swallowed and forced himself to peer between his fingers.

Amber eyes glittered in a face entirely covered in gray fur. Black fangs gnashed, and sharp claws tore at the grass. A sharp mineral odor like damp soil gusted from the beast's heaving nostrils.

She glared at him, her fury hot as golem's breath. In an instant, her claws struck him across the jaw. He felt them tear his skin, and blood dripped down his cheek.

"How dare you come here, human! How dare you trod on the sacred ground of spirits!"

He pressed a hand to his cheek. "P-please, the Queen—the token—she gave—"

But before he could squeeze the words from his frightened lips, the branches of the willows stretched out and snatched him from the ground.

"Stop! Leave him alone!"

Calliope raced toward the pond. She watched, helpless, as the trees flung Prewitt high into the air and hurled him violently down into the water.

He struggled and thrashed against them, but the trees showed no mercy, forcing him under again and again, the buttons on his jacket flashing in the moonlight.

The Guardians at the edge of the pond looked on in stony silence, like mourners at a funeral.

"Princess, wait," hissed Ilsbeth. "Wait! You must not—"

But Calliope ignored her. She raced on as fast as her legs would carry her, leaving Ilsbeth behind.

"Stop!" Calliope screamed. "I command you!"

The beast's flashing amber eyes turned toward her, but Calliope didn't care.

She ran into the water, wading out toward Prewitt, but just as she reached him, the branches grabbed her and flung her back onto the bank. From the center of the pond, Prewitt choked, gasping for breath before he was dragged under again.

"Who are you who dares to command the Spirits?" seethed the beast.

Calliope shoved herself up, running back into the water. She swam to Prewitt, wrapping both her hands around the branches; then she pulled with all her might, willing them to let Prewitt go, and to her surprise, they did.

They recoiled from her touch, and Prewitt splashed down into the water.

Calliope helped him to the bank.

He fell to his knees, vomiting into the mud. He coughed and coughed, and Ardal cleared his throat, relieved. No one had wanted to see the boy die. It was one thing to cast him out, to let the trees deal with him, but it would have been another thing entirely to stand by as he died on Glade ground.

The Guardians watched the newcomer crouch beside the boy, taking his face in her hands. The Wild Woman had listened to her. The trees had let the boy go. It was impossible. They looked at one another. *Who was this girl?*

"Are you okay?" Calliope asked.

Prewitt only nodded as he tried to catch his breath. Finally, he said, "You shouldn't have come here! You should have stayed—"

A loud hiss cut him off.

Calliope glanced up. The Wild Woman had physically recoiled from the pond, her fur standing on end.

The Guardians drew their axes.

There, floating at the center of the pond, was the black conch shell.

17

"Leave us," snarled the Wild Woman.

There was a moment of hesitation, the air thick with uncertainty, but finally the Guardians turned and disappeared across the knolls.

The Wild Woman bobbed her chin slightly, and the conch shell floated toward the bank on a lily pad, nudging the reeds, which lifted the shell into the Wild Woman's claws.

Calliope and Prewitt glanced at each other. The shell must have slipped from Prewitt's pocket during the battle with the willows.

The Wild Woman held it up in the moonlight. "A thousand years have passed since I heard the words held within this shell." Her voice was round and ancient, and the trees shivered around them. "The child had just called the Firebird back to

Lyrica. Spirit magic was renewed, our powers stronger than ever, and hope had blossomed where fear was all that had been. Nature was returned to order."

Calliope brushed the wet curls from her forehead, the moonlight snagging on the token she wore on her finger.

The Wild Woman continued without pause. "The girl had done what we could not. She had somehow held hope in her heart amid so much darkness and called the Firebird back to Lyrica. Because of her, the Demon was defeated. We were grateful. We were willing to swear our fealty to her and to accept the new magic the Firebird created—one built on a connection with humanity."

"The Feather," said Calliope.

The Wild Woman's eyes narrowed. "Yes. The Feather." Her face darkened. "I believed. I championed the girl. I opened the Glade and allowed the spirits of all things that grow beneath the sun to blossom and thrive for humanity. For a time, we were equal. We were friends.

"When my brother Spirit brought the prophecy before us, I was furious. How dare he bring us such a message when 'The Firebird Song' was still in the air? When peace had only just settled over the realms? But he was an Ancient Spirit of the mountains, of stones and rock, unchangeable. For him, the pain was still too fresh. His twin Spirit had been turned by the Demon and lost forever."

She lifted the conch shell up, and the voices poured from the lip, chilling the night air.

For to a child our fates are tied
If from the ashes she does rise
If perfect hope she can achieve
Then all that's broke may be redeemed

But if she fails, then all will fall
Mankind and spirits one and all
Shall share the shroud of pain and shame
Endless sorrow, fear, and flame.

Her claws silenced the voices. "It was enough to divide us. Some believed that humanity's hope would endure; the others insisted they were destined to fail and that when they did, we would be doomed alongside them—our destinies tied through the Feather. They left us and went across the Lyrican Sea to the Nymph Isles, where they could hide and forget. They abandoned us to our fates."

"But it's a prophecy of hope as much as doom," said Calliope. "How could they give up so easily?"

"Should they have put their lives and the lives of the lesser spirits at risk for *ifs*?"

Calliope scowled. "You said yourself that the girl had done what spirits failed to do."

"Yes. *One* girl did. But generations of other Queens failed. Humanity failed—as it always does—and the Demon rises yet again. Over and over. A promise of change and a return to suffering. Where does it end? Do not forget that it was humanity who welcomed the Demon into the realm in the first place."

She licked her fangs. "I should have joined the others, should have known humanity would forget and return to their ways, but I was naive. I believed entirely in the child's hope and in the legacy she would give to her descendants. But look around you!" Her voice rose, and the trees creaked on their trunks. "See what my choice did! These willows were once beautiful. But now they are shells, hollow and spiritless. Their souls were torn from them, and one by one their heart's blood drained into the earth."

Brambles rose suddenly around the pond, thorns stabbing, slicing into the ground, and Calliope tensed.

"Men came and ravaged the place that welcomed them. They cut down the trees, ripped up the roots of the living things. They wore branches like crowns and used my daughter's bleeding bark to soothe their own wounds. They called it *divine right.*"

All around, the trees groaned, and the Wild Woman's fury was palpable. "They did it all in the name of their Firebird Queen—a descendant of the girl who had promised to always keep 'The Firebird Song' in her heart."

The Wild Woman's amber eyes locked on the token on Calliope's finger. "I know who you are, Princess of Lyrica. It was *your* mother who allowed the Feather to be stolen without an alarm being sounded. Your mother, your very line, is a symbol of all that is wrong with humanity, of their forgetfulness, of their return to fear and chaos again and again—no matter their promises or intentions."

Calliope couldn't keep the tears from her voice. "I'm sorry." She had no right to cry. "I'm sorry that those men were so wicked. I'm sorry that other Queens broke their promises and that people forgot and did terrible things."

The Wild Woman gazed at her. "All that time alone in the dark. Could it really have made you any different?"

Calliope lifted her eyes. "I want to be," she said, staring deeply into the amber pools shining before her. She reached out a hand and laid it on the fur of the Wild Woman's arm. "Please," she said. "Will you help me? Do you have my mother's token?"

"Yes," said the Wild Woman. "I do have a token. But I will not give it to you."

Prewitt opened his mouth to say something, but Calliope shot him a glance, and he closed it again.

"You will have to earn it."

"How?" asked Calliope.

The Wild Woman's eyes flicked up to the moon. It hung bright and full above the Glade, illuminating her ageless face.

"The moon may seem to be shining, but it is only an illusion. She has no light of her own. She merely reflects the brightness of the sun gleaming beyond the desert in kingdoms you have never seen."

She held the shell out to Prewitt, and he took it quickly, tucking it back into his pocket. Then she turned toward the water, holding up her palms.

The lily pads drifted to the edges of the pond, lining the banks like bewitched spectators. The frogs stopped croaking, the crickets were still, the loon called out one last time, and then all was silent. The Glade hovered, waiting. The surface of the pond was so perfectly smooth that it was impossible to be certain which world was the reflection. Was the moon still up above in the sky, or had it sunken to lie at their feet?

The Wild Woman continued. "But the moon can reflect more than light. She also reflects events from the past, things she's seen with her wide and honest face. When the moon is full, and if she is willing, she might allow you to wade into her reflection and travel across her moon memories."

She held out her hand, letting moonlight rest in her palm. There, in the center of her open hand, blossomed a pale white moonflower. It opened, capturing the silver light in its petals.

"I have hidden the token in one of these memories. Find it and return. But be wary." The Wild Woman dropped the flower, and it floated a moment before sinking beyond their sight. "For a moon memory is a dangerous place, full of shadows and light. Step into darkness, and you will be trapped forever in the night of time past."

The Wild Woman turned to Calliope. "Princess of Lyrica, if you can prove that you are indeed different, that your eyes are capable of seeing what is truly important, then you will have your token. If not, then I am not to blame. The failure is yours alone, and I will accept whatever may come."

Calliope and Prewitt glanced at each other.

"But how will we know where—" Calliope never finished her question.

The words were snatched away by the branches that suddenly wrapped around her, lifting her into the air, then flinging her down, down, down into the moon's reflection. High above, the Wild Woman's frown vanished in a tilting blur of water and moonlight.

18

For a moment, there was nothing but moonlight.

It swirled around and through them, filling them up and pouring them back out. The light whirled into shapes of people, of moments, of time captured and held in the moon's memory.

And then, at last, it was over, and the children were standing knee-deep in frigid water, fractured ice nudging at their legs.

"Wh-where are we?" Calliope's teeth chattered as they moved toward the beach.

Prewitt looked around. It was a place he knew well, but it felt foreign.

He had stepped into his book of maps, back in time to when the city was bright and the castle was shining.

The moon's light poured down the city tiers from where it

floated above and behind the castle. Prewitt stared up at the starry sky, marveling at the way the millions of tiny lights sparkled. He wondered which one was the patron star.

"Are we home?" asked Calliope. It felt strange to ask such an obvious thing, strange that she didn't know what her own city even looked like—what her own castle looked like.

Prewitt nodded. "But it's not like the home I know. This is different."

Fireworks exploded across the water, and a cheer came from the crowded tiers.

Something nudged Calliope's leg, something floating on the surface of the slushy waves. She bent down, lifting it gently with numb fingers. It was the moonflower the Wild Woman had dropped into the pond. The delicate petals shimmered, weighed down with frozen sea-foam. "I've seen this flower before."

"Yeah, we both did. Just now. In the Glade."

"No." Calliope's teeth chattered. "Before that."

"You probably read about it in a book or something," said Prewitt, distracted. "Now, come on. Let's get out of the water and find you some boots before your toes freeze."

They waded past two children giggling as they dared each other to plunge in the icy water.

Prewitt paused, and Calliope turned. "What is it?"

"They can't see us," he said, waving his hand in front of their faces.

Calliope tried, too, but no matter how they waved, or jumped, or shouted, they got no response.

More children shrieked and laughed, chasing one another across the beach and along the tiers, golden crowns on their heads and imitation feathers in their hands. None of them had noticed Calliope and Prewitt's sudden appearance in the sea.

The ice-crusted sand crackled beneath their feet as they moved toward the boot locker, and Prewitt reached out and pulled on the handles. But when he opened the doors, he frowned.

Where normally there were shelves and shelves of boots, there was nothing but darkness—not shadow but a complete void of utter black nothing.

Confused, Prewitt reached out his hand to feel into the darkness, but Calliope grabbed his arm. "Wait!"

He glanced at her.

"Look." She pointed up the cliffside.

There were patches of black nothing all across the tiers. Where normally there might be shadows, people vanished, disappearing completely before reemerging in the light.

"Something isn't right," said Calliope. What had the Wild Woman said? *Step into darkness, and you will be trapped forever in the night of time past.*

She bent down and picked up a small white shell, covered in frost. Pulling her hand back, she tossed the shell into the boot locker. There was no clatter, no sound at all.

"Where did it go?" asked Prewitt, dumbfounded. He peered into the locker, but there was nothing but blackness.

Calliope shook her head. "It's as if it's disappeared

completely—no, wait! Prewitt!" She pointed down at her toes. "It's back!"

Sure enough, the white shell had reappeared exactly where it had been before she had picked it up.

"I don't get it," said Prewitt. "What does it mean?"

Calliope tugged on a curl, looking out at the water, at the stars shining above. "What if . . . ?" She paused. "What if the moon only remembers what its light touched? What if anything in shadow can't be part of its memory at all? Like it never existed."

Prewitt played with the buttons on his jacket. One was missing, and the cuff of his sleeve was torn. "But the shell came back."

Calliope paced across the sand, trying to work it out in her mind. It felt important to know the rules before they went any further. Not knowing could be disastrous. Why *had* the shell come back?

"Maybe the memory is like a story," said Calliope, squeezing eyes shut as she thought it through. "The words are in place. The ink is dry. But you and I aren't really a part of it. We're just the readers. We can try to change a word in our minds, but it belongs where the author already placed it."

Prewitt rubbed his freckles. "So anything we do won't actually change anything."

"I don't think so," said Calliope.

Prewitt looked around, picking up a driftwood stick coated in rime and breaking it across his knee. Then he tossed one end back to the sand and flung the other as far as he could into the sea. It splashed down into the waves.

A moment later, the stick reappeared, whole and renewed, exactly where it had been before.

"Firebird feathers," said Prewitt. "It's like magic!"

Calliope laughed. "After everything we've seen, *this* is what impresses you? A stick?"

Prewitt scrunched his brows. "But what about the locker? Where are the boots? They should be a part of the story, right?"

Calliope pulled on a curl. Back in the Cavern, she'd spent so much time lost in the pages of books, dreaming of other worlds and adventures. It had been safe there, a game. In her imagination, she always won, was always the hero. But here, the stakes were real. All of Lyrica depended on her getting this right.

When she finally spoke, she was careful, and the words came slowly. "In a story, there are always things that are hidden from the reader. The author doesn't show you everything. They might mention passing a door, but if they don't open it, you'll never see inside. Here, in the moon memory, the moonlight itself is the author. We can only see what it shows us, but anything else will never be part of the story. Not really. It's just blank parchment, like, say, the *inside of the boot locker*."

"To the new Princess!" A shout drifted down from a tier above, and a cheer rose, so loud that the gleaming lantern at the top of the Firebird Tale and Tome seemed almost to vibrate. "To the Princess!"

Calliope forgot about the shadows as she realized what the cheer meant. "They're talking about me," she said. "This must be the night of the Terrible Thing."

She looked up toward the castle, bright and cheery with candlelight in the windows. Somewhere, within one of those windows, her mother was still alive.

She rushed toward the steps.

"Wait! Where are you going?"

"To find my mother. I have to see her, Prewitt. Just once. How much time do we have? How long before the Spectress comes?"

"I don't—" Prewitt paused. He'd been about to tell her he didn't have any idea how much time they had, but then he remembered something Granny Arila had said. It felt like such a long time ago.

He pointed up at the sky. "See those stars? The ones in a row closest to the moon?"

Calliope glanced up.

"They're called the Six Seeking Sailors. Granny Arila told me that the last thing she saw before a black cloud covered the moon for good was the sixth Sailor reaching the top."

"But the second one's already there!" said Calliope.

Prewitt chewed his lip. "We might not have time to find your mother *and* look for the token."

Calliope's face scrunched. "We have to! This might be my only chance. I just want to see her face and hear her voice. Just for a moment."

Prewitt shifted. "All right," he said. "But we'll have to hurry."

She threw her arms around him, squeezing him tight before turning and racing toward the dark shadow at the base of the steps. She stopped when she got there, realizing there was no way around it. "What are we going to do? We're trapped on the beach!"

Prewitt swallowed. "Maybe if you run fast, the darkness won't hurt you. You said we're not part of this, right? So nothing can happen to us, can it? We're not really here."

Calliope huffed, her breath a cloud in the night. "The Wild Woman made it fairly clear that things *could* happen to us here," she said. "I guess there's only one way to find out what. We have to send something into the shadow that doesn't belong in the memory." She untied her sash, her shirt billowing in the sea breeze.

With a deep breath and a glance at the Seeking Sailors, she flicked her wrist, sending the end of the fabric into the darkness.

It hung, suspended half in the void and half in the moonlight, but when Calliope tried to pull it back, it did not come. She leaned, tugging with all her might, and for a moment, she was certain the sash would tear, but at last it gave.

She fell backward into the frozen sand.

They both stared at her sash. The part that had gone into the darkness had turned black and hard, as if it had petrified, and when Prewitt reached out to touch it, it disintegrated into the sand at their feet.

"Well that's . . . not encouraging," said Prewitt.

Calliope pushed herself up, frustrated. "We have to find a way over the shadow! Once we get onto the first tier, we'll be mostly in moonlight."

Prewitt looked up. She was right, but at the far edge of the sky, out in the distance, across the trees, he could see the stars winking out one by one as if they were being erased. The cloud of smoke was nearing.

"Cal," he said, choosing his words carefully. He was about to tell her that it was too dangerous to go to the castle, that there wasn't time, but he couldn't tell her not to see her mother while she had the chance. He couldn't imagine what it would be like never to have seen your mother's face. He would give almost anything to see his own mother, and he had seen her every day of his life.

"Maybe, if we build a ramp," he said, "we can walk above the shadow."

"Yes!" said Calliope. "Let's try!"

Prewitt looked around for something they might be able to use. In *his* Royal City, the sea was always dragging in driftwood, piling it up against the bottom tier. No one ever bothered to move it, and he had often climbed up and down the debris instead of taking the steps.

He looked around for a piece of driftwood that might be long enough, and once he found it, he and Calliope rolled it close, then worked to lever it up onto the step.

They tried over and over again, neither one giving up no matter how many times it slipped into shadow and dissolved back to its original place. It was frustrating, hard work. They tried not to be distracted by the stars, moving around the moon, and finally, they got the log balanced.

"Run!" shouted Prewitt, and before either one of them could think of the danger, they dashed up the driftwood. Prewitt's back foot slipped as the driftwood dissolved, and Calliope yanked him up to the safety of the bottom tier just as the log disappeared.

For some reason, the realization of how close he'd come to falling into the shadow made Prewitt laugh. Calliope covered her mouth, and they both giggled nervously as they dodged and dashed their way up the steps, trying to avoid the stretching and shifting shadows.

"Candied apples! Candied apples! They may not be golden, but they taste all the better for it, and they won't cost you but half a bivalve!" shouted a burly man, scarf wrapped around his head.

They ran past stalls selling freshly popped corn, spun sugar, and little cakes fried and topped with winter berries. Others sold souvenirs, portraits of the Queen, and gowns that had once been worn by royalty.

There was so much to see, and Prewitt wished they could take their time, but it was too dangerous to stand in one place with the crowd all around them, and the cloud of smoke was coming nearer.

When they finally made it to the top of the steps, they were careful to stay out of the castle's shadow. They weaved through the orchard where a narrow path of moonlight lay between the back of the castle and the trees, which were coated in shimmering ice that glittered and sparkled in the night.

Two men stood in the moonlight, their heads bowed close together, voices low and serious.

Prewitt and Calliope stopped short. One of the men was wearing a red jacket just like Prewitt's.

"Meredith!" cried Calliope. The men didn't react.

"Let's get closer," said Prewitt. "I want to hear what they're saying."

"Are you certain, Bookkeeper?" Prewitt's father asked, his voice trembling slightly. "Your spies could be wrong. They could be misinformed."

"I assure you my information is reliable," said the Bookkeeper. "The Demon is awake, and its servant is coming. The Queen and the new Princess are in grave danger, as are any of us who get in the way."

"What can we do?"

"You must go at once and warn the Queen. Somehow this is all connected to the stolen Feather."

Meredith tugged on his mustache. "We've looked everywhere, but whoever stole it has vanished."

"It's too late for that anyhow. The damage has been done." The Bookkeeper rubbed his head. "We need *real* answers. I'm going to the Nymph Isles."

"You can't be serious! The Nymph Isles? You'll never return! Besides, what good would information do us now, even if there were some way to get there? You said yourself it's too late!"

"Do not trouble yourself with that. My mind is made up. I sail within the hour."

The Bargemaster pulled off his cap. "If things are as bad as you say, then I must go and warn my wife. My son has only just been born. She's in no state to—"

"No, your wife must take care of herself. It is your duty to protect your Queen. Now, I must go and change the city lantern before I leave. Something terrible is coming, and Lyrica may not make it through the night." Without another word, the Bookkeeper swept away, back across the orchard.

For a moment, Prewitt's father remained where he was; then he took a deep breath, pulled his cap back onto his brow, and disappeared through an archway and into the void beyond the moonlight.

Prewitt swallowed past the lump in his throat. He had always thought his father cared more about duty than he did about him, but in that moment, Prewitt had seen the struggle play across his father's face, and he realized that it wasn't that simple.

"Come on," said Prewitt. "Let's find your mother."

A long row of arched windows along the back of the castle shone, the moon's face bright in the glass.

"How do we know which one is the nursery?" asked Calliope, but no sooner had she asked than the trees creaked and bowed, and a figure appeared suddenly in the treetops.

Prewitt and Calliope stared at each other. It was the Wild Woman in her beast form.

She leaped from the trees, and vines spread out from the castle, catching her and lifting her up. They flung her at one of the windows, and she smashed through the glass with a scraping of claws.

They heard a shocked cry, but it was swallowed almost immediately by a raucous cheer from the tiers.

Prewitt turned to Calliope. "I guess we know which one is the nursery."

19

"**Are you sure you want to do** this?" asked Prewitt. "Are you sure this is something you want to see?"

"Of course I'm sure," said Calliope. She grabbed the vines and began to climb up toward the window where the Wild Woman had vanished. She had missed her mother her entire life, but when Meredith had told her the truth of how she had died, of how she'd been *murdered*, the missing had turned to mourning.

Now that she was here, she knew she couldn't leave without taking something for herself. She needed one memory of her own.

She climbed up to the window ledge, steadying her nerves as she peered down into the nursery.

Moonlight poured through the empty pane, streaming across the carpet and shining onto the white canopy. Someone shifted beneath it, and Calliope tensed. She held her breath as two bare feet slid from the blankets and a face turned to the window, curls shining in the moonlight.

"Mother," whispered Calliope. Her heart drank in the moment, letting it seep into every vein like liquid gold.

She was draped in a long velvet robe, and in her arms, she cradled a baby.

"That must be you," said Prewitt, climbing up beside her. "Strange, isn't it?"

The Wild Woman's furry head floated beneath the broken window, the rest of her body eaten by darkness. "You *must* call the Firebird back," she snarled.

The Queen shook her head. "I can't. I don't have the Feather."

"You lie!" hissed the Wild Woman. "I can feel its power, faded but here. Do not try to hide it from me."

The Queen frowned. "That's impossible. It was stolen, I assure you. There's no trace of it, nor of the Thief."

"So you've lost the only hope we had." The Wild Woman's words were bitter as she reached into the fur at her chest and pulled something out, brandishing it in front of her. It was a root or a branch of some kind, black and rotting.

"The Glade is dying. The Demon is awake. Even now, hope is draining from our world."

"Then it's true." The Bargemaster stepped into the light. "The Bookkeeper was right. The Queen is in danger."

The Wild Woman hissed. "Always thinking of yourselves. We're *all* in danger!"

The Queen held the baby out toward the Wild Woman. "I know you won't help me. But won't you help her? Take her back to the Glade. Keep her safe."

The fur at the scruff of the Wild Woman's neck rose. "I will not bring a *human* to the Glade," she spat. "I will not help you at all. If you die, good riddance. I only came for the sake of the other spirits."

The Queen took another step forward, holding out the baby. "Please. She's innocent."

"Innocent! She is human. She can never be—" The Wild Woman broke off. Bright green shoots stretched from the tip of the dead branch, and a white flower blossomed in the moonlight.

Prewitt leaned forward, nearly falling from the windowsill. "Cal," he whispered, "did you see that?"

Calliope nodded, eyes wide.

The Wild Woman's voice softened. "*To a child our fates are tied.*"

The Queen's eyes lifted. "What did you say?"

The Wild Woman began to pace. She moved back and forth beneath the windowsill, her claws snagging the rug. Finally, she turned. "The girl must go to the Sacred Cavern. It is the only other place that is safe from the Demon's eye, the only place where the original magic of 'The Firebird Song' is still strong. But be warned, if the Demon's servant were to seek it and find it, it might not hold. Secrecy is the key to the child's survival. She must stay hidden until she reaches the Age of Hope. *Twelve years.*"

The Queen shook her head, holding the baby to her chest. "So long!"

"Only then will she have the ability to call the Firebird back," said the Wild Woman. "The girl is the only chance we still have to keep the Demon from regaining full power. If that happens, the Firebird will never return and all of us, spirits and humans alike, will be cast into darkness for all eternity."

The Queen's face was grave. Her emotions tugged at the corners of her eyes and pulled at her cheeks, but after a long moment, she nodded and turned to the Bargemaster. "You have to take her, Mer."

He shook his head as the Queen pressed the infant into his arms. "No. She must stay with you."

The Queen stood up straighter, grabbing the Bargemaster by the arms. "You have to do this, Mer," she said. "You must take her and keep her existence a secret, even from those closest to you. You must keep her safe at all costs until she reaches the age when she can do what I have failed to do. The entire kingdom depends on this."

"But what about you?" Desperation trailed sweat across the Bargemaster's brow. "I won't leave you behind."

"You must. Meredith, if what the Bookkeeper told you is true, if the Demon's servant is really coming tonight, then we have no time to waste. I failed, Meredith. *We* failed. This is our chance to do the right thing. I must do what I can— whatever I can—to convince the Demon's servant that she has already won."

The Queen bent and heaved back the corner of the rug.

"Whoever she is, she will never expect a new mother to leave her child. I will make it seem like the Princess is still here with me. It might be enough to give you a head start."

The hatch winked up at them.

"Please, Carmina, don't throw your life away."

"I'm not. I'm making it matter."

Meredith's mustache trembled. "At least let me take the baby down to one of the women in the city. She will be happier there. My wife would gladly—"

"Do not argue with your Queen," snarled the Wild Woman. "If the child is to be untainted, if her hope is to have any chance at all, then she must be hidden away from the fear that is about to darken Lyrica."

The Queen looked at Meredith. "Promise me," she said. "Promise you'll keep her safe. Promise you won't let my sacrifice go to waste."

Meredith pressed three fingers to his lips. "I promise."

Prewitt saw the pain twist his father's face and knew how difficult that promise had been to make. He had accused his father of doing nothing on the night of the Terrible Thing, of abandoning his duty, but he could see now that his father *had* done his duty in spite of the pain it caused him.

The Queen leaned over, kissing the baby's forehead. "Goodbye, my darling Calliope. Be brave."

"Cal?"

"What?" The word was like glass in her mouth, and the tines from the golden ring dug into her palm. It was all too much to bear.

"The fifth star is almost to the top of the moon. We have to go. We have to find the token." Prewitt waited for her to react, to nod and agree that they needed to hurry. But sorrow covered her eyes like clouds.

"Calliope?"

"You go."

"What? No! Not without you!"

"I'll come in a minute. I just need a little more time."

"There isn't any more time."

Prewitt's words were weighty, but they made no impression. Before he could stop her, Calliope jumped down from the windowsill and fell into the nursery.

"Watch out!" said Prewitt, and Calliope realized just how close she'd come to landing in the shadows.

But the danger didn't feel real. It didn't feel urgent. Everything was dimmed by her mother's presence. *She* was what mattered, what was truly important.

Calliope turned. The Queen had collapsed on top of the hatch, her curls hiding her face. "Will she be all right? Please, Wild Woman, I have to know."

Calliope walked toward her, kneeling down beside her. "I'm all right, Mother. I'm here." Calliope wrapped her arms around her mother's shoulders and pulled her tight. She breathed in the scent of her hair, felt the softness of her skin, and she wished more than anything that her mother would hug her back.

Prewitt wasn't sure what to do. They were running out of time.

The sky glowed suddenly red, and there was silence as the revelry on the tiers cut off. Then the entire city screamed at once. The Bookkeeper had changed the lantern. It was the signal to flee to the cove. Something terrible was coming.

"Calliope," he said, and he knew his voice sounded pitiful, but before he could say anything more, before he could plead with her to come with him, the fireplace exploded.

The Queen slipped from Calliope's arms, scuttling away from the billowing smoke and sparks.

"It's the ash golems!" shouted Prewitt, and for a moment, the shock woke Calliope. She jumped up, shedding ash from her pants legs.

But it was not the ash golems at all.

A person unfolded themselves from the fireplace, batting the flames from their cloak as they staggered from the grate.

The Wild Woman stepped forward. "Who are you?" She reached out a claw, hooking the hood and lifting it from the figure's head.

The face was illuminated fully in the moonlight.

The Queen gasped, and Calliope took a step backward, bumping into a gilded mirror on the wall.

Prewitt thought he might be sick. He pushed his head out into the fresh air.

"What has happened to you?" asked the Wild Woman, curiosity sweetening her voice.

The face was charred so badly, it was impossible to tell

whether it belonged to a woman or a man. The skull was hair-
less, the flesh melted to reveal bone. The nose had been burned
away completely, the lips peeled back from the teeth, and the
left eye socket was empty and gaping.

The figure's breathing was ragged and shallow, and they
reached a shaking hand into their pocket and pulled out a fist-
ful of gleaming golden fragments.

Calliope recognized them at once. "Prewitt!" she said.
"The tokens!"

Prewitt whooped. He could have wept with relief. "Take
them, and let's get out of here!"

Calliope nodded, reaching out and grabbing them from the
figure's charred hand. She held them up, beaming at Prewitt,
and they glittered in the moonlight. But before Calliope could
slip them onto her fingers, they dissolved back into the figure's
palm.

It was in that moment, standing with a handful of nothing,
that Calliope realized suddenly that everything around her was
an illusion. A dream. A memory of things that she could never
truly have.

She had let herself be swept into the moment, swept into
wishing, into wanting things to be different, and so she'd
forgotten why she had been sent into the moon memory in the
first place.

The Queen pressed herself to her feet, looking closer at
the fragments. "What are they?"

"Can't you see? It's what remains of your Firebird Feather," said the Wild Woman wryly. "I told you I could feel it here. Your Thief has returned."

"Cal!" Prewitt said. "Did you hear? The Thief! It's the Thief!"

The word jolted Calliope from her daze, and she shared a look with Prewitt. *Wind. Woman. Thief.*

The Queen shook her head at the charred figure. "This can't be the Feather! What have you done to it?"

Calliope tore herself away. Even if they hadn't found the Wild Woman's hidden token, they now knew what the Thief looked like, and that was something! She moved toward the windowsill, and Prewitt sagged with relief, but Calliope suddenly stopped. Her face drained of color.

"What?" said Prewitt. "What are you waiting for?" He followed Calliope's gaze. Neither of them had noticed the shadow creeping farther and farther from the base of the window.

Now, more than half the nursery had been taken over by black nothing.

Their eyes met, and they both knew without speaking a word. Calliope was trapped.

"Maybe you could jump," said Prewitt, but it was a hollow suggestion. A jump that far would be impossible.

She looked around the room, desperately trying to find another way out. The shadow was growing by inches now. The Wild Woman disappeared into the darkness, her voice the only evidence that she was still there.

"The Feather is destroyed, but there may yet be magic

within it. See how the fragments glow? It may still be enough to call the Firebird back when the girl reaches the Age of Hope."

The shadow forced Calliope farther and farther into the room. The Wild Woman had told her that she would have to prove that she could see what was truly important, and it was clear now that she had failed. She had let her feelings get in the way, had let her sorrow and yearning keep her from doing what was best for the kingdom.

"We must separate the fragments, hide them until the Princess is old enough to search for them."

"Please . . . ," the Thief rasped. "Do not make me take one. Let me die. I've come only to try to set things right."

"You will not die," said the Wild Woman, not a trace of sympathy in her voice. "You will suffer, and your body will rot, but you will not die. Not until what has been broken is repaired. That is your curse. The cost of what you have done. You dared to steal hope."

"I had my reasons."

"Your reasons cannot save you now. You will take a fragment, and you will keep it safe until the Princess comes for it."

There was a long pause, and then the Thief said, "I will take it and hide it in the last place the Spectress would ever expect to find it. I will return to the mountains."

"So be it," said the Wild Woman. "Now, go. Back the way you came."

There was a sound, like the rustling of clothing, and then the Thief was gone.

"Cal," Prewitt called, stress straining his voice. "The sixth star is almost to the top."

Calliope felt panic sweep across her. "You have to go without me! Otherwise you'll be trapped here, too."

Prewitt shook his head. "I can't leave you!"

The Wild Woman's voice rang out. "I summon you, South Wind, stealer of secrets. I summon you to keep this great and dangerous secret, this token—a piece of the Firebird Feather."

Wind gusted around the room, blowing back the curtains and rustling the vines in the window. The shadows spun around the room, and Calliope screamed, ducking and dodging, trying to avoid them. "You have to go!" She yanked the token off her finger. "Take this. Maybe you can still find the last one. Go to the mountains. Find the Thief. Maybe it will be enough." She flung the token toward the window, and Prewitt nearly fell, but he managed to catch it.

"Cal, I don't—"

"Go!" The dark cloud had come into view beyond the pane, and Calliope could see the stars near Prewitt's head blinking out.

With a final glance over his shoulder, Prewitt slid from the windowsill.

Calliope crouched in the last patch of moonlight. There was nothing she could do now. The entire room was in darkness, but for the glowing window high above.

"Please, Wild Woman." The Queen's voice shook. "Won't you hide the final fragment? There is no one left but you."

"I've done enough. Beyond this room, beyond this moment, my help will come to an end. It will be up to the girl to prove that she is worthy."

"But—"

"This fragment will remain here, in this night, caught in these moonflowers."

Calliope reached into her pocket, feeling the petals of the moonflower she'd plucked from the edge of the sea. She remembered now why the flower was so familiar. She and Prewitt had seen the same flowers blooming in the nursery, thriving in the wreckage. She could picture the place where the planter had been, but now it was buried in darkness.

"We're out of time," said the Wild Woman. "The Demon's servant is coming. I can feel it. There is nothing I can do for you now."

The Wild Woman suddenly reappeared in the window, wrapped in vines.

With a jolt, Calliope realized that the beast's form was about to block the moon.

She looked desperately for somewhere she might be safe, but it was too late—the room was thrown into darkness so complete that Calliope forgot the memory of light.

It wasn't just darkness. It was silence, silence so absolute that it felt like a physical force.

Calliope couldn't feel anything at all, not the rug beneath her feet or the chill air on her cheeks. She tried and tried to feel anything besides the black weight, a sense of urgency welling within her, but there was nothing but nothing.

She focused on her fingers, tried to remember how they felt, pushing harder and harder, refusing to give up, and finally, she sensed the briefest brush of something smooth and cool at her fingertips.

The petals of the frozen moonflower.

With all her effort, she lifted her arm, which felt as if a thousand anchors weighed it down, and to her shock, she found that she could *see* the flower. It was shining, giving off a light of its own, radiating gently from each petal, and for a few inches on every side of the flower, she could see through the dark.

Calliope could have wept with joy, but she knew that she mustn't lose her focus.

She was still in the nursery, but all the color had drained from the room. It was smeared with grays and blacks that reminded Calliope of the wreck it would be in the future.

She saw her mother, moving in slow motion, lifting a black storm glass from the mantelpiece and flinging it at the rug. She picked up a shard and swiped it across her palm, blood streaming in a black streak.

Calliope wanted to run to her, to give her one last hug, but instead she pushed through the darkness and shadow, her fingers tight on the flower. She waded toward the planter and saw more moonflowers glowing, radiant and white. She reached down, feeling through them, searching for the Wild Woman's token—for the fragment that she now knew was a piece of the Firebird Feather.

There was no way to tell how long she stood there, searching through the flowers and dirt. Time was like the colors, faded and unreal, and when she finally found the token, three words were shining black on the castle wall, and her mother was standing by the bassinet, a heap of blankets cradled in her arms.

She was saying something that Calliope could not hear, and a tear fell down her cheek. Calliope fought the desire to stay, to be with her in these final moments. Her mother shouldn't have to die alone.

But she already had. The ash golems had already come. The Spectress had already written this part of the story, and no amount of wishing could unwrite it.

With all her effort, Calliope turned away. She had to look forward, to the future, to Lyrica.

She raced down the city steps, no longer caring about the shadows. She charged through them, the flower in one hand, the token in the other.

She saw Prewitt waiting at the water's edge. He looked like he was struggling to decide what to do, taking one step toward the water and then turning back and glancing up at the castle.

He shouted and nearly toppled over as Calliope burst from the shadows, flinging her arms around his neck. She collapsed against him, her shoulders shaking, and she wept with relief for what they had gained and sorrow for what she had lost.

Prewitt's cheeks flushed. He wasn't sure what to do, what to say that could make any of it better. "It's okay," he said, patting her back. "We'll find the token some other way. You're safe, and that's all that matters."

Calliope stepped back, wiping her cheeks. She held out her hand and opened her palm. The Wild Woman's token gleamed in the moonlight.

"You did it!" he said, amazed. "How?"

"I'll tell you later," she said, and she slipped the token onto her finger before grabbing his hand.

They ran into the water and sloshed into the moon's reflection, falling down, down, down. They sank into the moonlight, and the last thing they saw before the water and light swept them away was the dark cloud gulping down the moon.

20

"But you have to help us!" Calliope stood, dripping between the elm rows. The Guardians sat impassive on the curved bench before her.

The Glade Girls were gathered to one side, their faces giving nothing away.

There had been no sign of the Wild Woman when Calliope and Prewitt had trudged from the pond, but the Glade Girls had been waiting across the knolls.

"We did it." There had been no triumph in Calliope's voice. "We found the Wild Woman's token. Now we only need the Thief's."

She was wrung out from the moon memory, weighed down by the heaviness of seeing her mother. She had thought it would make her feel better, having a memory of her, but somehow it made everything worse.

Still, she had to push on. She had to make her sorrow matter. She had to save Lyrica.

Calliope had turned to the Glade Girls. "We need your help. We can't go to the mountains on our own. We need the Guardians and the Wild Woman."

Ilsbeth had shaken her head. "They will not help you, Princess."

The words were another blow, but Calliope had refused to give up.

Even now, as she stood in front of the stern-faced Spirits, having heard the words straight from Ardal's lips, she couldn't accept it.

"You have to help!" she said again. "If not for us, then for yourselves. Didn't you hear what we told you? The fragments *are* the Feather. We can repair it. We can fix what has been broken. We can call the Firebird back and restore everything!"

"You must give us time to determine the best course of action and how that action may affect the Glade. We must take a few months to—"

"We don't have months!" said Calliope, stamping her foot.

She turned and pointed at the Glade Girls. "They fought ash golems today! Right here, within your border."

The Guardian beside Ardal humphed. "Ash golems *you* brought."

Ardal lifted a finger, and the Guardian was silent. "You say that the last fragment is all you need, but the Queen must sing the Song of Hope as well. Do you know the Song?"

Calliope bit her lip. "Not yet, but—"

"So even if you found the fragment, if you restored the Feather, you would be no closer to calling the Firebird back. Yet you ask us to risk ourselves, to go where the Demon might speak to our hearts. We have seen it before: spirits lost to fear."

"You wouldn't be—"

Ardal held up a hand. "You do not have the knowledge required to defeat the Demon. Without the Song, you are just a girl."

Calliope's head whipped toward Ilsbeth, but Ilsbeth refused to meet her gaze.

Calliope gritted her teeth. "I am not *just* anything. You underestimate me because you think I don't know enough! But I have gotten this far!" Calliope was trembling, her face bright red. "I am the daughter of the Firebird Queen."

"You are the daughter of generations of Firebird Queens who forgot what mattered, who caused pain, and sorrow, and suffering. I have always championed humans, but how can I still after what they did to the Glade? After the Wild Woman opened our borders and taught her lesser spirits to trust, only to have that trust be so horribly broken? Humankind did what they always do; they forgot their promises. They destroyed nature that had grown for them. They conquered and pillaged instead of simply enjoying and honoring what the Wild Woman had given them. They broke her heart."

Calliope didn't know what to say.

"I do not mean to be cruel," said Ardal, his voice gentle. His hand rested on the fox's head, and it pressed its cheek into his palm. "You are young. You do not have the memories that we do. You have not felt the sorrows of thousands of spirits or heard their cries as they suffered. Still, you must face your weakness. You will never be the *first* Firebird Queen. However, I will allow you to stay here with the Glade Girls where you will be safe."

Calliope looked again at Ilsbeth and the other girls. They stared straight ahead, stone-faced.

Ardal continued. "The boy, of course, cannot stay. We will give him guidance through the woods, and he will return to the Royal City."

Prewitt pulled his hands from his pockets. "I can't go back to the Royal City! It's my duty to be here! I'm the other half of the moon! The prophecy says—"

"How dare you!" Calliope exploded, and everyone between the elms turned to look at her. The full force of her glare was turned on Ardal, and even he was startled. He had never been shouted at by a human before.

"How dare you talk about safety! You don't want to keep me safe. You don't care about me at all. If you did, you would listen to me. That's part of being a good leader, isn't it? But you're too stuck in your own beliefs. You're stuck in the past. You say I don't have enough knowledge. Maybe you have too much!"

The moonlight shone on her furious face, and for once, Ardal was the one with nothing to say.

Calliope went on. "You blame me for all that has happened. But I wasn't even alive. You've been here the whole time, but you refuse to accept any of the responsibility. The Feather bound humans and spirits. That makes us equal! You aren't the only ones who have suffered. We are suffering, too. On the way here, I saw a little boy, and he was *starving*! Starving! While you sit here in the Glade and do *nothing*." Her voice rose, and Prewitt felt it again, the power that he'd sensed when she had summoned the Wind.

"You call yourselves Guardians!" she shouted. "But who is it you're protecting?"

"We protect the Glade and all its inhabitants," said the man beside Ardal.

Calliope snorted. She walked to the nearest elm, grabbing a piece of the bark and stripping it off. It came away easily, and the inside was streaked with black rot. "Is this *protection*?"

She went on down the row, tearing back the outer skin of the trees. Black sap oozed, and the stench was fetid and sweet. The Glade Girls looked at one another, and the Guardians shifted in their chairs.

Calliope turned back to Ardal. "Stay in the Glade if you like. But I will find the Thief, and I will call the Firebird back with or without you, and once again, Lyrica will be saved by a little girl while *you did nothing*."

Calliope whirled. "Come on, Prewitt. We're leaving." She stomped toward the edge of the trees, Prewitt in tow.

"Wait!" Ardal got to his feet, and the men beside him stood as well.

Calliope turned back, and there was something in Ardal's eyes that surprised her: it was awe.

21

The Glade Girls spun and struck, their whips cracking. Leafy bundles of water sailed toward jars of fireflies hanging from cords in the trees.

Glass exploded all at once, and swarms of fireflies floated up to rest in the branches above.

Calliope tried to focus. She tried to pay attention as the girls showed how to drop their whips into leather pouches of water at their waists and exchange them for fresh-soaked, pliable cords.

She tried to push away the fog of disappointment as Ilsbeth demonstrated how to peel the leaves from the willow branches before plaiting and soaking them in water to keep them from becoming brittle in the face of fire.

Ardal and the Guardians had promised to prepare them for their trip to the mountains, to share as much knowledge as they could, and to make sure they were well supplied. But that was where their help ended. They still refused to accompany them, to go anyplace where the Demon might speak to their minds.

"If the Demon turned us, we would be a powerful weapon for its cause. We will not risk it."

That was what Ardal had said, and it wasn't entirely unreasonable, but it still felt like an excuse. Calliope couldn't feel grateful. The Spirits should be doing all they could. After all, it was their world, too.

Fi showed them how to sew the little leafy pouches using tiny silk stitches that made them watertight. She dipped one into a bucket of water, letting it swell before lifting it out and closing the stitches.

"We have spent our lives training, just in case the Spectress's monsters ever broke through the Glade's protections," said Ilsbeth. "But until this afternoon, we had never seen one."

"Really? It looked like you knew what you were doing," said Prewitt, fumbling as he tried to coil the whip the way he'd been shown.

Ilsbeth's eyes could have pummeled Prewitt to the ground. "We *do* know what we are doing."

"We didn't mean to bring them here," said Calliope quickly.

"How *did* you get here?" asked Hazel.

Calliope told them about the patron star and about the bell. "We were desperate. The ash golems attacked, and we didn't know what else to do. We thought the star would take us home. That's what the book said, but instead, it brought us here."

"That's because your seafarers got it wrong—as usual."

They looked up. Ardal stood above them, his arms crossed.

He had been listening to their conversation, and he couldn't help but interject. *"Our patron star shall guide us home, if hope can call it with a tone."* He smirked behind his massive beard. "Humans are always trying to explain how spirits work, but they care more about rhymes than accuracy. The lesser light spirit that you call your patron star doesn't guide anyone *home.* It takes ships back to the place of their births."

"But the *Queen's Barge* wasn't built here," said Prewitt. "Was it?"

"I thought you said you were the Bargeboy," said Ilsbeth. "Do you not know?"

Prewitt flushed, but before he could answer, Calliope spoke. "Of course he does. I think what Prewitt meant to say was that it wasn't *entirely* built here, right, Prewitt?"

Prewitt nodded, shoving his hands in his pockets.

Calliope sat up straighter. Meredith had told her the story of the *Queen's Barge* time and time again. It was one of the few stories he told himself instead of simply bringing a book.

"The Barge was made after the first Firebird Queen was crowned, while 'The Firebird Song' was still in the air. It was supposed to be a symbol of hope and new peace, so the people who lived in mountains forged the golden figurehead and the fog bell, and the river tribes brought gemstones for the eyes, and the desert nomads brought glass for the carriage, but the wood was the most important of all. It came from an ancient tree that was cut down in the Halcyon Glade. That's why the star brought us here. Because timber is what makes the heart of a boat."

Ardal's mouth twitched behind his beard. "Now you've got it."

Calliope smiled at him, but then she caught herself and let her smile drop. She didn't want him to be nice to her. She wanted him to go with them to the mountains and help them defeat the Spectress.

Ardal cleared his throat, suddenly uncomfortable. "That's enough training for the evening. It's time to go and get some supper. You've all earned it."

"You should not be so hard on him," said Poppy after Ardal had walked away.

"I just don't understand why he won't help," said Calliope. "He won't leave the Glade! He acts like he cares, but if he really cared, he would do something. At least the Wild Woman hid a token; at least she took you in and kept you safe."

"It was not the Wild Woman who saved us," said Fi.

"But I saw the notes in your trunks."

"Yes, our parents wrote to her because they believed she might have mercy, and they knew that it is her magic that protects the Glade, but it was Ardal and the Guardians who saved us."

Calliope's head turned to where Ardal and the other Guardians were sparring in the moonlight at the edge of the training grove, axes and broadswords clanging. She watched the fox shadow Ardal's heels, and she felt guilty for her anger. Whatever his failings, he had taken pity on the girls, had taken them in and risked the Wild Woman's wrath, and that counted for something.

For a moment, she wondered what would have happened if her mother had left her at the edge of the woods with a note.

Would she have grown up here with the Glade Girls? Would she have learned to fight? Would she have been a part of their family?

They stood in unison, coiling their wet whips and tucking them into their pouches. Fi had said she was their sister, but watching them, Calliope knew she was separate.

"Let's go and eat," said Hazel. "It's late. We can train more in the morning."

Calliope and the Glade Girls left, but Prewitt decided to stay behind and train longer.

Ilsbeth held out a whip.

"You're staying?" he asked.

"You cannot train yourself." She looked on with folded arms and disapproval as he practiced.

He tried again and again, ignoring the grumbling of his stomach. The first time he connected with the glass, he whooped and dropped the whip, but the jar only swung gently in the branches.

Ilsbeth barked corrections at him and demonstrated over and over the proper way to hold the whip, but the longer he tried and failed, the more irritated she became.

"Not like that! Like this!" There was a loud *crack* and glass exploded, fireflies rising up in a glittering cloud.

Prewitt tried again, but no matter how he tried, he couldn't quite seem to get the hang of it.

"There is no hope for you if you can't manage something this simple!" hissed Ilsbeth. "How are you going to keep the Princess safe? You are slow, and clumsy, and you do not know how to use weapons at all. You flinch like a coward every time the whip cracks."

Prewitt felt heat rising into his cheeks, and his hand tightened on the whip. "You think you're so much better than me just because you know how to fight. But I'm not the one who has been hiding in the Glade for the past decade. You'd never even seen an ash golem before today."

Ilsbeth shoved her whip back into the pouch at her side, water sloshing out. Her face twisted, and her jaw was tight. "I have been training," she seethed. "I have given every moment of my life, every hour of my days, to becoming the best fighter I can. We all have."

"So what?" said Prewitt. "It isn't like you've offered to help us defeat the Spectress. What good is fighting if you won't use it to help anyone but yourself?"

"It's called *survival*. But what would you know about that? You're just a boy. You don't even have a right to be scared—the Spectress isn't stealing little boys from their beds."

Anger stung Prewitt's eyes. "Say what you want about me, but it's better to be a coward and try than to be brave and do nothing at all. I'm doing my duty whether I'm scared or not."

Ilsbeth glared at him a long moment. "*The other half of the moon*, is it?" She scoffed. "You must have gotten the prophecy wrong. It cannot mean you. You want to do your duty? Then leave. She will be safer without you."

With that, Ilsbeth turned and walked away, the jars of fireflies swinging gently behind her.

22

Spoons froze on their way to mouths, hovering over bobbing dumplings in steaming broth as Ilsbeth stormed into the kitchen cottage.

The moon shone through the branches that formed the roof, a pattern of shadows like lace across the table.

"Where's Prewitt?" asked Calliope.

Ilsbeth told them what had happened, and Calliope shoved her chair back, jumping to her feet. "How could you say that, Ilsbeth? How could you tell him to leave?"

"I did it to protect you."

"I don't need protection," spat Calliope. "I need my friend."

"Are you so certain he *is* your friend?" said Ilsbeth. "Did he say that? Or is he here because he thinks he is the *other half of the moon* and it is his *duty* to help you?"

Calliope ran from the cottage.

"Prewitt!" She called his name into the night, but only her voice came back to her.

When she got to the training grove, it was empty.

She searched, growing more anxious as the minutes passed. Of course Prewitt was her friend. How could Ilsbeth suggest that he wasn't? They had been through so much together. Calliope decided that when she found him, they would leave. There was no point in staying where people judged and refused to help.

She shouted across the shadowed hillocks. When she got close to the pond, she slowed. Prewitt wouldn't have gone near the willows, would he?

"Prewitt?" she whispered.

The boughs rustled.

Calliope.

Calliope stopped among the reeds, peering through the black-limbed copse. "Prewitt?"

Calliope.

The hairs on her arms stood on end. "Who's there?"

Calliope.

Her pulse thrummed in her temples. She looked around. Across the pond, she saw the Wild Woman watching her. The Ancient Spirit was beautiful beneath the trees, serene, and stately, and inhuman. Her presence made Calliope shiver.

"I thought I heard someone calling my name," she said.

"Yes."

"For a moment—" Calliope broke off. She wasn't sure she

wanted to say it, but she pushed on anyway. "For a moment, I thought it was my mother."

She had heard her mother utter only a few words, but it had been enough to etch the sound of her voice on her heart.

The Wild Woman watched with luminous eyes. She reached out a delicate hand, beckoning, and Calliope hesitated.

"Come," commanded the Wild Woman.

Calliope swallowed and moved around the edge of the water until she stood beside her. She could feel the Spirit's energy like a chill on her skin.

"Look into the pond." The Wild Woman pointed.

Calliope gazed out at the water, and at once she saw that something was not right. The surface no longer reflected the stars. It no longer shone with the brightness of the moon. It was a black pit. Staring into it was like staring into the Nymph Isles storm glass. There was nothing to see, nothing at all.

She glanced up at the Wild Woman. "I don't understand. Is it another moon memory?"

Calliope, where are you?

Calliope's breath caught. "Mother?"

She knelt by the edge of the pond, reaching out, but just as she was about to touch the black water, soft-headed reeds nudged her hand away.

"She is beyond your reach," said the Wild Woman. "Beyond my vision, beyond even the moon's vision."

"Then why can I hear her?"

"The roots of the Halcyon Tree grow beneath all realms.

Here in the Glade, we are the closest to its roots, and so we are connected to the other realms, even the ones that cannot be walked by the living. On occasion, the water of the pond acts as an amplifier and voices or images slip through."

My daughter.

Calliope blinked. She didn't want to be here anymore, didn't want to hear her mother's voice. All it did was cause her pain. What good was hearing the voice of someone who could never hug you, could never see you? She hid her face in her hands.

"Do not hide from your sorrow," said the Wild Woman, and she lifted Calliope's chin with a gentle finger.

"She died for me," said Calliope. "So I could have a chance."

"It is awful to have someone you love torn from you, to have their life taken. But it does no good to blame yourself. Guilt will not bring them back, and sorrow will do nothing but steal your energy."

For a moment, they were silent in shared loss.

"Tell me, who is to blame for the death of your mother?"

Calliope kept her eyes on her toes. "I am," she whispered.

"No!" The branches of the trees clawed the ground, flinging up black dirt.

"Do not answer with sorrow! Answer with rage! That is where you will find the truth. Who is to blame for the death of your mother, Princess of Lyrica?"

Calliope's eyes lifted. *"The Spectress."* The name was steel on her teeth, and she felt the fury of it sharpening her senses.

"Yes," hissed the Wild Woman. "Because of her, you grew up friendless in the dark. Because of her, you were weaned on fear and caution. Because of her, you will never know the true feeling of a mother's comfort. Let that knowledge drive you. Let righteous fury fill you and propel you to *action*. That is true hope."

Calliope nodded slowly. Hope and fury did feel very much the same. They were emotions that inspired action, where guilt and sorrow had only weighed her down and taken away her sense of purpose.

In the Barge carriage, Meredith had warned her not to act out of anger, had said that it would make her reckless. But he hadn't *wanted* her to take action. He had wanted her to stay safe and alone in the Cavern.

The Wild Woman smiled for the first time, dimples burrowing into her cheeks. "There is no greater hope than fury," she said. "The willows that surround you were watered with the blood of the men who wronged me. Tell me, what man would dare cross me now? That is *real* power."

Calliope shivered, and she felt a warning thrill through her. She couldn't forget that the Wild Woman had refused to do anything while humankind suffered. She had refused to help even the most innocent infant. What had begun as a rage against wrongdoing had turned into something different, something selfish. Even now, Calliope was certain that if she asked the Wild Woman for help, the Spirit would deny her.

I must never let my anger keep me from doing what is right, she thought. *I must use it carefully, like a sword, to protect those being harmed, to stand up to what is wrong, but I must never, ever let it make me cruel.*

The Wild Woman stood. "The pond has gone clear again." Sure enough, the moon and stars were shining once more in the pond's surface. The whispering was gone, and the sounds of the night expanded.

"I have to go and find Prewitt," said Calliope. "I've stayed here long enough. It's time for us to go to the mountains and find the final token."

She looked at the Wild Woman and took a chance. "The South Wind told me that I was not the only child hidden in the dark. It said there was another girl kept prisoner in the mountains, one with the Demon's Mark. Do you know who she is?"

The Wild Woman shrugged. "I cannot keep track of all human children." She tilted her head, her silver bangs tangling in her lashes, and for a moment, it looked like she was going to say more. But Calliope never found out for, at that very moment, she heard someone scream, and flames ignited across the knolls.

23

Prewitt sat in the Barge carriage feeling sorry for himself. Ilsbeth was right. He was useless. He was a coward. He was small, and he couldn't fight. Why had he ever thought he could help? Just because some prophecy had said he could?

But that didn't seem fair. He hadn't known about the prophecy when he'd decided to find Calliope. He had gone because of what the ash golems had done, because of his mother's tears, because there was no one else and he had promised Granny Arila he would follow his destiny.

But he didn't even know what that destiny was—not really. He had found Calliope. Was that his only role? He had brought her to a safe place. Maybe Ilsbeth was right; maybe now he was just in the way. If he weren't there, maybe the Glade Girls would even help her, and maybe the Wild Woman and the Guardians would, too. Maybe it would be better for everyone if he just went home.

Prewitt missed his loft bed, falling asleep with the smell of damp hay in his nostrils. He missed the sound of the rain pinging the bucket and the rumbles of his father's snores. He missed his mother most of all.

He had never appreciated his home before, but now, feeling small and useless in the middle of a place where he wasn't wanted or welcome, he wished he were back.

He scowled at himself in the cracked glass of the carriage door. His face was dirty, and his jacket was torn and missing buttons. He looked nothing like his father now. He wiped his nose on his sleeve.

Prewitt had been so angry with him, had thought him a coward for doing nothing when the world was in danger. But now he knew that his father *had* done something. He had kept the Queen's secret, had kept the Princess hidden—even from his family. The Queen had ordered him to take the Princess to safety, and even though it had clearly pained him to leave the Queen behind to die, his father had obeyed because it was his duty.

Prewitt played with his buttons. That *was* the reason, wasn't it? After all, his father talked of duty constantly. What other reason could there have been? His father had sacrificed his own desires for what the Queen had said he must do. But Prewitt had seen the pain on his father's face, had felt the sorrow, and he had known there was something more than duty there, even if he wasn't quite sure what.

Ilsbeth had said that the Princess would be safer without him. Was leaving what he was supposed to do, even if he didn't want to?

When Calliope had stepped from the shadows of the moon memory, he had felt more than just relief. He had promised himself he would never let her send him away again. He would stay with her. He wouldn't let anything happen to her.

But what if staying put her in more danger?

Beyond the glass, something shimmered.

He pushed open the door, walking out onto the quarterdeck. Crickets chorused in the night.

He leaned over the rail, looking down onto the row deck.

The two crescents glowed gently through the thick layer of soot that coated the slats. Prewitt walked down the steps and stood in front of the symbol, staring at it.

There it was, shining up at him, the certainty that he needed. The symbol had appeared for him and him alone—the moment he stepped onto the deck with Calliope for the first time.

Maybe Ilsbeth was right. He was small, and he was scared, and he wasn't very good at fighting or knowing things. But as long as he was the other half of the moon, he would stay—no matter what Ilsbeth said.

He tugged his jacket down and was about to jump over the gunwale and head back to the village when he saw something flickering in the dark. Prewitt squinted, peering out into the night. For a moment, he comforted himself with the thought that he was only seeing fireflies in the branches a long way off, but then he realized the truth, and his breath caught.

Ash golems. They were moving stealthily, not igniting

anything in their path, their mouths shut tight to hide their molten bellies.

Prewitt crouched, peeking over the railing. They were close. He could hear them now. But he was hidden behind the gunwales. If he was very quiet, if he didn't make a sound, they would pass by. He would be safe. But everyone else . . . *Calliope.*

It was not duty that made him scream. It was something stronger. *"Ash golems! Ash golems! Ash golems!"*

There was no more stealth. The monsters blazed to full brightness, swirling and rising, blowing out fiery breaths in all directions, igniting the grass, and the daisies, and the trees.

The Barge lit, too, a slow burn from the base, hit by at least a dozen golems at once. Prewitt felt it crumpling, sinking as it turned to ash, but he did not stop screaming.

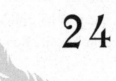

24

Calliope knew at once who was screaming. She didn't stop to think. She jumped to her feet and raced toward the sound of Prewitt's voice.

The Wild Woman leaped up, too, darting across the surface of the pond on feet that shifted to claws. She passed Calliope, her streaming hair shrinking to fur as she bounded toward the expanding orange glow.

Calliope ran faster than she ever had before, adrenaline taking over. The Glade Girls converged on her, gowns streaking behind them, whips out.

The Barge was a torch in the night, and it drew them all, monsters, and girls, and furious spirits.

The carriage frame crumpled and screeched, a dying creature on a pyre.

"Prewitt!" Calliope screamed, stinging eyes raking the wreckage.

"There he is!" shouted Ilsbeth. "Near the firebird!"

Calliope saw him then, standing at the figurehead. He was still shouting, crazed and unseeing, the flames leaping up all around him.

"Go back to the village," ordered Ilsbeth. "We will handle this." She disappeared into the blaze, followed by Hazel, Poppy, and Fi.

But Calliope couldn't leave, not while Prewitt was in danger. She stood with her feet in a stream, watching as the Glade around her ignited.

The Wild Woman tore at the ash golems with teeth and claws, and the willow branches she wore grew and stretched like the whips the girls carried, ripping away ashen arms and legs.

Ardal and the Guardians spun, striking out with broadswords and axes, their movements a blur too fast to track. Sparks flew as ash golems broke apart and then re-formed again and again.

It was endless.

Calliope watched and waited for what felt like an eternity, but finally, Ilsbeth and Fi reappeared, swinging over the figurehead with Prewitt between them, Hazel flinging leafy pouches to clear the way.

The Barge groaned one last time and collapsed, black smoke filling the sky and smearing the stars.

Calliope tripped across the smoldering grass, her feet blistering. She flung her arms around Prewitt. His face was pale and streaked with ash, but he was all right.

"You warned us," said Hazel. She shared a glance with Lanna. "Even though it put you in danger."

Prewitt nodded. "I had to, otherwise everyone would have died."

A whip cracked near Calliope's elbow, and a golem exploded. Its head rolled on the ground at her feet as Ilsbeth flung leafy pouch after leafy pouch. Its smoking eyes stared, its mouth yawned, and finally it heaved a slow, shuddering breath of steam and stilled.

But it didn't matter. One fallen ash golem was hardly a nick in the Spectress's demonic arsenal.

The monsters were everywhere now, fed and strengthened by all there was to destroy. They rose by the dozen from the flames around the Glade, climbing out of flaming trees and ascending from sparking hillocks.

The Glade was lost.

"Retreat!" shouted Ardal. "Retreat to the willows!" He spun, the fox at his heels, and the Wild Woman followed.

The Glade Girls were at Ilsbeth's side.

The Barge was gone. It had burned quickly and now was unrecognizable. Something flashed in the firelight, and Prewitt saw the star glimmering in the ashes. The bell had survived. So had the firebird figurehead.

He plucked at his buttons. Was he still the Bargeboy without the *Queen's Barge*?

He felt Calliope step close.

"The only parts fire couldn't destroy were the parts made

in the mountains," he said, looking over at her. He saw the devastation on her face and knew she felt the loss of the Barge as much as he did.

"I'm sorry," he said.

Calliope's eyes blazed. "You have nothing to be sorry for. This is because of *her*."

The figurehead toppled, sending a galaxy of sparks into the night.

"Princess, you *must* come," said Ilsbeth. "The pond is the only place where we will be safe. The Wild Woman will take us into a moon memory, but we have to hurry, before the smoke covers the moon's face."

Calliope shook her head. "I'm not running away, Ilsbeth. I'm going to the mountains for the last token. It's the only way to stop this."

The girls looked to Ilsbeth, waiting. She shifted, her hand tense around the whip.

"Come with us," pleaded Calliope. "Help us stop the Spectress, and you can all go back to your families."

"Ilsbeth has no family," said Hazel.

Calliope blinked. "Then who left you in the woods?"

"No one," snapped Ilsbeth. "I crawled into the trees on my own."

"We can't stop the Spectress," said Hazel. "Look around! She has beaten us already! The Guardians and the Wild Woman are running away. What can we do that Ancient Spirits cannot? We are just girls. "

Calliope looked hard at Ilsbeth. "I know *you* don't believe that, Ilsbeth. You said—"

"It does not matter what I said. I follow my sisters."

Calliope looked to the other Glade Girls, but they avoided her eyes.

"If you believe that, then you've already lost," spat Calliope.

"Girls!" shouted Ardal.

Nearly all of the Glade was burning now. Even the village blazed in the distance.

The moon was growing hazy overhead.

"Go," said Ilsbeth. "Run into the woods at the south side of the Glade. They the only one not burning. If you can make it there, you may have a chance."

She pressed a green whip into Calliope's hand and then turned and ran toward the pond, the other girls on her heels.

"Ilsbeth!" shouted Calliope. Ilsbeth stopped, turning to look over her shoulder. The others continued running. "You act like you aren't their leader, but you are. They think this is what you want, but none of them will be happy trapped in a memory. You want to be free as badly as I do. You *want* to fight. Isn't that why you've spent your life training?"

Ilsbeth's face contorted, and for a moment, she seemed to lose control of her emotions, but the moment passed, and her face was itself once again.

"I trained because I want to *survive*."

She turned and fled.

Prewitt didn't know if Ilsbeth could hear him over the sound of the dying Glade, but still he shouted.

"You think I'm a coward, but you're the one running away!"

Prewitt and Calliope fled into the trees. The sudden change in temperature was shocking, cool air needling their steaming cheeks. Branches grasped, thorns scraped, and everything was utterly dark and silent.

Calliope whirled, looking back the way they'd come. Somehow, she still believed that Ilsbeth and the Glade Girls would follow, that they wouldn't just leave Lyrica to her fate, but there was nothing behind her but thick, gnarled forest. Even the smell of smoke was gone, replaced by the heavy scent of sodden pine and decaying leaves.

"I can't believe the Glade Girls didn't help us," she said, her voice hollow.

"Who needs them?" said Prewitt. "You and I are fine on our own. Two halves of the moon, right?"

Calliope tried to smile. She was glad Prewitt was there. She would have been afraid if she'd been all alone. Still, what Ilsbeth had said bothered her more than she wanted to admit. Prewitt wasn't there because he was the other half of the moon, was he? They *were* friends, too, weren't they? She didn't know why it mattered so much to her, but it did.

Calliope stepped forward, squinting to see between the gnarled silhouettes. "But where did the Glade go?" They must be only a few steps beyond its borders, but all traces of it had vanished. The only evidence that it had ever existed remained in Calliope's and Prewitt's memories.

Now, there really was no choice but to go on. On toward the mountains.

Rain drenched in sloshes as it spilled from the canopy, and Calliope wiped her eyes. She was about to ask Prewitt which way he thought they should go when she heard him gasp.

She spun around, but before she could make out more than a flash of steel, something struck her on the side of the head, and she fell down into rotting leaves and darkness.

They had run away from the Glade and straight into a trap.

25

Prewitt's face slammed into steel armor over and over again, bruises blackening bruises, but the pain was nothing compared to the guilt that pummeled him.

He should have known—should have been more cautious! Why hadn't it occurred to him that it was all a trap? That the golems weren't just there to destroy the Glade. They were there to smoke them out.

Before he had realized what was happening, before he could do anything to help Calliope, he had been hit over the head and flung upside down into a sack. He didn't even know if Calliope was nearby—if she was okay.

A man's rough voice broke into his worries.

"Keep the Princess's head out of the bog, you imbecile! The Spectress wants to kill the girl herself."

Prewitt tensed, biting his tongue. She was okay! For now. But time was running out. They had to find a way to escape.

They were crossing *the bog*. Prewitt remembered it from his book of maps. It lay at the foot of the mountains, the volcano rising above, the river winding along its eastern edge.

He could smell it now, foul and gripping, like the inside of a wet and well-worn boot. He could hear the buzzing of a million gnats and the slapping of steel gloves against cheeks followed by spats and curses as the men were bit and bothered.

The sounds of the footsteps suddenly changed, no longer squelching but striking something hard like slate, and he knew they were entering the mountains. He tried to think past his pounding head, tried to keep track of the turns, drawing them out like a map in his mind. His memory might be their only chance of finding their way out again.

"I thought we were taking them to the caldera," said one of the marauders. He sounded like he had a cold.

"No, you moron. The Spectress isn't here. She went to watch the Glade burn. Wasn't going to miss that little pleasure, was she? Been trying to find it for years. It wasn't until that Barge got in, taking a couple of her ash golems with it, that she was finally able to *see* inside."

The boots tramped on for a few minutes, until a sickening stench suddenly wafted through the burlap. Prewitt nearly gagged.

"I hate this corridor," said the sniffly marauder.

"Boo-hoo for you. This is the only way to the dungeons."

"But there's something rotting behind that door. Can't you smell it?"

"Don't talk about that door. Don't even look at it."

"Why not?"

"Don't you know anything? That's where they locked *her* up. No one's allowed near it. Not ever."

Prewitt craned to hear more. *Her?* Could they be talking about the *marked girl?* Hadn't the Wind Spirit said she was a prisoner in the mountains?

The guards stopped talking, the funk faded, and soon, he was shaken out of the bag onto the hard floor of a cell. A wrought iron gate slammed shut with an echoing *bang*, and the boots stomped away.

Prewitt lay perfectly still until he was certain the men were gone; then he sat up, searching for Calliope.

He found her, not too far away, and for a moment, his heart turned to lead so heavy that it weighed down his limbs until he couldn't move, not even to call out.

But then she groaned and opened her eyes, pressing her fingers to her temples. "Ouch," she said.

"Cal! You're okay! Thank the Emperor!"

"Where are we?"

"We're in the mountains," said Prewitt.

"Oh," said Calliope. "Well, at least it's where we wanted to go anyway." She didn't sound particularly enthusiastic. She stood up, wobbling a bit.

"But there's more," said Prewitt. "I heard something." He told Calliope about the door the marauders had passed and about their strange reactions. "Then the man said, *That's where they locked* her *up.*"

"*Her?*" Goose bumps swept across Calliope's arms. "He said *her*? Are you sure?"

Prewitt nodded.

Calliope tugged on a curl. "They have to be talking about the marked girl!"

Prewitt grinned. "That's exactly what I thought! Cal, what if we're *supposed* to set her free? What if the Wind's secret was actually a clue and we didn't even realize it?"

Excitement flushed Calliope's cheeks. Since she had heard the girl's cries and the odd, metallic music, she had wanted to do something to help her. It had bothered her to know that someone was being kept in the mountains, but she had told herself there was nothing she could do until after she had found the tokens.

What if she'd been wrong? What if it was all linked? The marked girl and the tokens?

"The prophecy," she said. "It mentioned her! I don't know why I didn't think of it until now. *Twelve years to suffer / Twelve years of hate / The Demon's Mark will seal our fate.*"

Prewitt whooped. "Cal! You're a genius! If we free her, I bet it will change everything! I bet she's supposed to help us find the final token!"

Prewitt reached through the bars, trying to grab hold of the lock on the other side, but it was bolted high on the stone, far above the ceiling of the cell, attached to a post that had to be lifted out and turned to release the door.

The sound of rushing water reverberated around the

dungeon, and hot mist drifted across the cell, carrying the stench of sulfur.

They peered through the bars at the far end of the cell. The stone floor continued a few inches beyond before suddenly dropping off. Down below, the river raged and churned its way through the mountains, coughing up billows of steam.

"I guess we're not getting out that way," said Calliope.

"Prewitt?"

Calliope and Prewitt stared at each other. Neither one of them had spoken.

"Firebird feathers! Prewitt, is that you?"

They turned and ran to the door.

Across the aisle, a boy in a too-big waterman's jacket pressed his round face against the bars.

"Jack?" said Prewitt, not believing his eyes. "What in Lyrica are you doing here?"

26

Mist had wound its way through the streets as Jack and the watermen trekked up the city steps toward the falconry.

"I'm certain Smith's falcons will be able to find the Halcyon Glade."

"I don't know," said Old Harry. "The Falconer might not help us."

"He will once I tell him the Princess survived. He was always loyal to the Queen before. There's no reason that should have changed."

"Shouldn't we be telling *everyone* that the Princess survived?" Jack asked. "Why keep it a secret?" He felt giddy, alive in a way he hadn't felt before. Maybe this was what hope felt like. He'd been too cautious to ever allow himself to find out. "Everyone will want to help us find her!"

Old Harry shook his head. "No, son. You saw what happened with Granny Arila. People are too afraid to get involved."

Jack chewed on the end of his braid. He had been afraid, too, but knowing for sure that the Princess was alive had made all the difference.

A man slept on the steps, his beard full of grime, and the watermen stepped over him.

Jack bent down, pushing his shoulder.

"Gidoffme." The man rolled over.

"Leave him, Jack," Cedric called over his shoulder. "He'll sober up enough to stumble back to the tavern in an hour or two."

Jack reached into his pocket, pulling out a piece of salt-fish. Then he leaned down and whispered in the man's ear. "The Princess is alive! We're on our way to find her. She's reached the Age of Hope, and she is going to call the Firebird back." His heart sped up as he waited for the man's reaction.

"Jack!"

Jack tucked the fish into the man's hand and ran on.

They stood in the doorway of the falconry, rain splattering mud onto their shins. Spirit chimes jangled, and Meredith reached up, silencing them before knocking.

"I have a bad feeling about this," said Old Harry.

Cedric rolled his eyes. "Come on, Harry. You're being paranoid. You've known Smith his whole life."

Old Harry shook his head. "The man I knew died a long time ago. He hasn't been himself since his wife was killed and his daughter was taken."

Jack tilted his head. No one had ever told him the Falconer had a family.

The words had barely left Old Harry's lips when the door was flung open.

The Falconer filled the doorway, a glaring peregrine gripping each leather-clad shoulder. His brows sunk onto his lids when he saw them, and he spat on the ground at their feet. "What do you want?"

Meredith stepped forward, pulling off his cap. "We need your help."

Smith folded his arms across his chest, he and his birds casting identical stormy glowers. "Why should I help you? We're not friends."

The chimes clanged in a catch of wind. Meredith lowered his voice and leaned forward. "*The Princess is alive.*"

The Falconer blinked, and in an instant, his demeanor changed. "Come inside," he said, beckoning them with a wave of his gloved hand.

The watermen and the Bookkeeper filed into the falconry. It was surprisingly warm and dry inside. Smith had pressed sea mud into every seam and crack in the walls, painted it thick beneath the hay that covered the floor.

"Where are all your birds?" asked the Bookkeeper, noticing the empty perches.

Smith cleared phlegm from his throat. "Getting some air. Now, tell me, where is the girl?"

He laughed when they told him. It was an ugly sound that sent chills up Jack's spine. He wished that the Bargemaster hadn't brought them here, but he knew that they didn't have any other options.

"*The Halcyon Glade*. So it's the Wild Woman to the rescue, is it? The monstrous murderer of men whisked the girl to safety, did she?"

"We don't know what happened," said the Bargemaster. He told Smith about the twin hourglasses and about the sparkling sand. "Where else could the sun still be shining? It's the only conclusion we can draw. "

Jack looked around. He'd never been inside the falconry before. He noticed a tin cup on the mantel, and he frowned. The cup was misting, like breath in cool air. He glanced at the others to see if they had noticed, but they were focused on Smith.

Smith's eyes narrowed, and he wiped a hand across his mouth. He glared at the Bargemaster. "I came to you, and you said you didn't know what happened to the girl. You said you had no memory."

Meredith shifted. "I was trying to keep her safe."

"Safe from me."

"Safe from all of this!" Meredith waved a hand. "There's never any break from it! Day in, day out, it's all the same. Fear, and death, and misery. How could anyone be happy living like this? How could anyone be hopeful *here*?" Meredith's voice cracked. "I had to protect her, to keep her hope as untainted as I could. I did it for all of us—whatever you may think."

Smith's mouth curved, but his smile was not kind.

The watermen glanced at each other. "Maybe we should go," said Old Harry.

Smith went to the window, flinging it open. Rain slanted, soaking the hay. He lifted a gloved hand to his shoulder, and

215

one of the remaining peregrines stepped onto it. Then he lifted his arm, and the falcon launched itself into the storm.

"Thank you," said Meredith.

Smith grunted.

"How long will it take it to find the Glade?" asked Cedric.

Smith responded, but Jack didn't hear. He had moved to the mantel to investigate the cup. He peered inside, and heat dampened his cheeks. He frowned. How could the drink be warm?

He glanced down. A wad of thick brown blankets filled the fireplace. He bent, heaving them aside.

"Get away from there!" snarled Smith, but it was too late.

They all saw the smoking coals.

The Bookkeeper staggered back. "Traitor!"

Jack hadn't seen Cedric draw a dagger. Maybe he'd had it in his hand the whole time. The blade was pressed against the Falconer's ruddy throat. "Tell us where you sent that bird, and while you're at it, tell us where all the others have gone as well."

The Falconer's eyes flicked to the Bargemaster.

Meredith shook his head. "No, Smith. Tell me you didn't."

"She promised me my girl. She says she'll give her back."

Old Harry pressed his hand to his forehead. "Firebird feathers, Smith. You would sacrifice the Princess for the possibility that the Spectress kept your daughter alive all this time?"

Meredith looked out the window. He cursed. "The marauders are back."

Old Harry turned to Jack, grabbing his shoulder. "Get to the water, okay, son? Just get down to the dory and row her out as far as you can."

The marauders surrounded the falconry.

Meredith pressed open the door, and they gathered on the stoop.

The spirit chimes whirled.

Metal fists raised as one, and Jack held his breath, but before the fists could strike down, something hit one of the marauders on the back of the head.

The marauder turned to see what had hit him. A piece of salt-fish lay in the muck. A man stood behind him, grinning. Jack couldn't believe it. It was the drunkard from the steps!

"Didn't you hear?" The man cackled. "The Princess is alive!" He scooped up a handful of mud and flung it at the marauders.

For a moment, they were all stunned.

Then Old Harry shoved Jack in the back. "Go!"

Jack took a deep breath, and he ran.

27

"I didn't make it to the boat."

Deep in the mountains, Jack pressed his forehead against the iron bars.

Prewitt looked down the aisle, searching the cells, eyes raking the shadows. He was afraid to ask, but he needed to know. "Jack, where is my dad?"

Beside him, Calliope tensed.

"I don't know," said Jack. "I haven't seen anyone else. Maybe they got away."

He looked at Calliope, blinking wide eyes. "Are you really the Princess?"

She nodded.

"I told you I'd find her," said Prewitt.

Jack tilted his head. "But why haven't you sung the Song yet? Why hasn't the Firebird returned?"

Calliope and Prewitt told Jack the whole story from beginning to end.

After they were done, Jack said, "When they brought me here, we passed a row of longboats near the river. If we can get out of here, I think we could escape with those; then we can go and find the last token together."

Prewitt shook his head. "We can't leave the mountains. The Thief is here."

"And the marked girl," said Calliope. "The one from the Wind's secret."

Jack nodded. "Okay, I'll help you find them. Let's just get out of here!"

It took some thinking, and some discussion, and several failed attempts, but finally they found the answer.

It was inside Jack's pocket, along with a mishmash of other less useful things—a scrap of netting. It was tangled with hooks and lures, and as soon as Calliope saw it, she had an idea.

She dug through her satchel and pulled out her silver shears, sliding them across the aisle. They scraped the stone as they slid, not quite making it all the way to Jack's cell, but he stretched his arm through the bars and snagged them with the tips of his fingers.

Prewitt whooped, and then he and Calliope watched, clinging to the bars, as Jack cut the netting and retied it so that it was one long piece of rope with knots all down it at various intervals. After that, he wrapped it around and around the post.

Calliope and Prewitt whispered encouragement, and after a few tries, leaning back as far as he could to help the rope grip, the post slid up a few inches. Jack was so surprised that he let go and had to start all over again. But finally, it worked. The post pulled up far enough that Jack was able to turn it. With a loud *clack* and a squeal of metal, the cell door swung open.

Calliope flung her arms around Jack as he set them free. "I'm so glad you were here," she said. "What would we have done without you?"

He laughed, and the sound was light and careless, at odds with the dreariness around them. "Who knew getting captured could be a good thing?"

They were about to leave the dungeon behind when Calliope noticed something in one of the cells at the end of the aisle.

At first, she thought the cell was filled with heaps of blankets, but then one of the heaps moved and another coughed.

Three girls lay on the floor in the damp.

Calliope rushed to push up the lock, but it was rusted, and she couldn't get it to budge. It took all three of them to finally get the door open, and they waited for the girls to stand up and leave the cell, but instead, they cringed back.

"Hurry," said Calliope. "You have to come with us before the marauders return!"

"Cal," said Prewitt, eyeing the girls. They were thin and pale, and none of them looked healthy. "If we take them with us, they'll slow us down."

"I don't care," said Calliope.

"We'll get caught."

"We can't just leave them here, Prewitt!"

Jack shifted. "I can do it," he said. "Let me take them to the boats. I can get them out of here."

"By yourself?" asked Calliope.

"Jack," said Prewitt. "The water is rough. How are you going to navigate it alone?"

Jack looked at Calliope, and then he stood up straighter, buttoning his coat. "I can do it," he said.

Prewitt tilted his head. "You're different."

Jack smiled. "I can see it now, Prewitt—the way things *could* be. It's because of her." He glanced at Calliope and then flushed, looking quickly away. "It's because of you, too, Prewitt."

"Me? What did I do?"

Jack smiled. "You believed. You went and found the Princess when nobody else would. You're the bravest person I know."

Prewitt watched, dumbfounded and lost for words, as the other boy stepped into the cell and crouched down. Jack thought he was brave, but Prewitt hadn't felt brave at all.

"Don't be scared," said Jack, holding out a hand to the girls. "I'm going to help you get out of here. Do you understand?"

Two of the girls hid their faces, but the third nodded.

Jack turned to her. "It's going to be dangerous, and I'll need your help. I'll need you to shout when the turns come or let me know if we're going to crash into something. Do you think you can do that?"

The girl shook her head. "We can't leave. She'll hurt us."

"You're already hurt!" said Calliope.

Another girl lifted her head. "It isn't that bad. We have blankets, and if we're good, they feed us."

Calliope felt the blood rush to her cheeks. She opened her mouth to say something, but Jack interrupted her.

"I used to think that trying to make my life better was too much of a risk. I thought I was being grateful by just accepting the way things were. But really, I was afraid."

Three sets of eyes lifted to his face.

Jack nodded toward Calliope. "Do you know who that is?"

They shook their heads.

"That is the Lost Princess of Lyrica. She is the daughter of the Firebird Queen. She is twelve years old—*the Age of Hope*—and she has come to the mountains to call the Firebird back and defeat the Spectress once and for all."

The girls' eyes were pale moons, full and bright.

One of them leaned forward, the thin blanket falling from her grubby shoulders. "I'm twelve, too," she said.

"Then that makes you the Age of Hope, too!" said Calliope. "That's the age when extraordinary things happen."

"But I'm still scared."

Jack smiled, glancing up at Calliope and Prewitt. "That's the thing about being brave. It's easier when you don't have to do it all alone."

They stood beside the row of gilded longboats. Calliope hugged each of the girls, and when she was done, she hugged them again.

"I'll see you soon," she promised. "Everything is going to be all right. You'll see."

Prewitt stood in front of Jack. "Firebird protect you, waterman," he said.

Jack's cheeks dimpled. "Waterman. I like that."

Calliope and Prewitt helped push the boat into the water and, standing shoulder to shoulder, they watched as it disappeared into the mist.

28

Calliope and Prewitt hurried through the mountains, their nerves on edge at every turn.

Each time they peered around a corner and found it free of marauders or ash golems, they sighed in relief.

Torches flickered nearby, and Calliope flinched. "Let's hurry. I'll feel better once we rescue the girl. Hopefully she can help us find a less conspicuous way to move through the mountains."

As they rushed onward, farther away from the dungeons, the caverns began to change. The dark and dingy walls brightened into a jeweled glow as the wealth and opulence that had once characterized the mountains oozed from the stones. The pavers beneath their feet shifted from rock to gold, and the walls shimmered with crystals of every hue. Gemstone-coated stalactites oozed from ceilings like chandeliers.

They were shocked when they stumbled into a cavern filled to the brim with forbidden items. Naked books with broken spines, lutes with strings hanging like bowels, harps melted into dejected lumps—everything was strewn together in giant heaps.

"Firebird feathers," whispered Prewitt, turning in a circle. There were so many things to see, things he had no names for, and he knew that if they'd had more time, he could have spent hours running his fingers over them all.

Calliope's eyes shifted across the objects, trying to read their stories. Each one had belonged to someone, had been loved and treasured, and each had been torn away and thrown like garbage into forgotten heaps.

She was so overwhelmed that she didn't pay attention to where she was stepping until her bare sole pressed hard on something small and sharp. She sucked in air and hopped around, holding her foot.

Prewitt bent over and picked up the squashed piece of silver. "What is it?" he asked.

Calliope scowled. "I'm fine, Prewitt. Thank you so much for your concern."

Prewitt ran his finger across the metal edge. "No, really, it sort of reminds me of the tokens."

Calliope sighed, leaning in. He had a point. Before the silver piece had been smashed, it might have been a similar shape to the rings on her finger, except that it was much longer. It even had little marks on the outside where at some point there might have been tines.

Prewitt tucked it into his pocket, and they crept on through the halls. Just as he was beginning to wonder if he'd misremembered the turns, the smell hit them. They covered their mouths, gagging, and when they rounded the next corner, they saw the door.

They might have missed it if they hadn't been looking for it. The door was made of the same rock that surrounded it, and the stone handle was all but invisible in the shadows.

A shout came from around the corner—"The Princess has escaped! Find her!"—followed by the clattering of metal boots on golden pavers.

"Get inside!" hissed Prewitt.

Calliope didn't have time to steel herself. She grabbed the handle and shoved the door open. They pushed it closed and leaned against it, choking on the rancid air. The smell was so intense that their eyes spilled.

Prewitt gagged and tried to keep from throwing up. Maybe the marauders had been right; maybe something *had* died in here. He was afraid to look.

A rat scurried across Calliope's toes and she squeaked, covering her mouth with her hand.

Across the room was a small bed, and on it someone lay in a heap, unmoving.

"Hello?" Calliope whispered. She stepped closer, but Prewitt pulled her back, shaking his head.

"I think—I think they might be dead," he said.

The heap shifted and then began to unfold.

Prewitt sighed. Not dead, then.

Calliope pulled away from him. "We've come to rescue you," she said.

A black cloak spilled down to the floor, and a dark hood fell back, revealing an oozing scalp that glistened in the dim light.

"I know who you are." The voice rasped from the figure like a ripped flag in the wind. "You have your mother's face, Princess of Lyrica."

Calliope frowned. It wasn't a child's voice at all. It was the voice from a memory—a memory of a memory. "You're the Thief," she said.

Time had not been kind to the Thief. The burns had not healed—in fact, they looked worse than ever. Skin rotted and dripped from bone. Where eyes should have been, there was only one, bloodred and bulging. Seeping cartilage was all that remained where a nose should have been, and a yellow maggot wriggled from the gaping hole.

Prewitt turned away, retching.

Calliope tugged her curls. The Wind had not said how long it had carried its secret, but looking around, it was clear that it had been many years since a child had lived in this room. A heap of metal toys sulked in the corner, covered in dust. Well-read storybooks lined a shelf blanketed in white cobwebs. A table near the bed was set for a tea party, the tiny cups and saucers lonely and faded.

You were not the only child locked away in the dark. There

*was another. She's still there, a secret prisoner of the mountains—
the one with the Demon's Mark.*

She lifted her eyes to the Thief's face. "*You* are the marked girl," she whispered. "That's why you stole the Feather, isn't it?"

The Demon's Mark will seal our fate

It had begun with a stolen Feather, and the girl had stolen it because of the Mark.

Her heart ached with sympathy. She couldn't imagine the suffering this woman had gone through. Of course she had wanted hope. Calliope couldn't even be angry with her.

The Thief groaned, crumpling back onto the bed. "Oh, no," she said. "I am not the one with the Demon's Mark."

"You aren't?" asked Prewitt.

"No, but I am her sister."

"But where is she? What happened to her?" asked Calliope. "We heard her cries in the Wind."

"Would you like me to tell you the story?"

Calliope nodded.

"All right." The Thief took a deep, rasping breath and then began.

"When my sister was born with the Demon's Mark, our father tried to kill her right away, but before he could, my mother named her. *Seraphina*, she called her, and then she died. She had known my father could not kill my sister after that.

"So he did the only thing he could do. He hid her here in this cave—"

228

"What did it look like?" interrupted Prewitt. "The Mark?"

"It wasn't like you would expect," said the Thief. "They never were. You would think it would be a blotch, or a horn, or a tail, but that was the trick of it, you see. The fear of it was insidious because no one knew what the Mark truly looked like. Whenever an infant was born with anything that could be considered an abnormality, even if it made them more beautiful, they were feared. To be a marked child was to be born *different*."

Calliope wanted to ask more, to know exactly what the girl's Mark had been, but the Thief had already gone on.

"My father saw it as a personal act of great mercy to let Seraphina live, but he was afraid of what would happen to him if she were discovered. He did not trust anyone to even deliver her meals, so I came myself twice a day. I brought her books and gifts." She waved a hand toward the toys in the corner. "I did everything I could to make her happy. But there was only one thing that could ever make her smile. A gift, crafted for her by our most talented Forgeman. He had a unique ability to see the heart of a person, and he made her the perfect toy: a rosewood box that played music."

Calliope and Prewitt looked at each other. They had heard the music in the Wind, the tinny tune mingled with the sounds of the child's sorrow. Calliope wrapped her arms around herself.

"She was obsessed with that box. It made her forget that she was unhappy. I even heard her chattering to herself, singing along as the box played. For a while, I think it was her way of escaping her reality."

Calliope's cheeks burned. She thought of her paper animals.

"Throughout the years, the Forgeman cast dozens of songs onto silver, and I brought them all to her." The Thief's mouth twisted at the memory.

Prewitt reached into his pocket, fingering the squashed silver piece. He lifted it out. "Is this one of the songs?" he asked.

"Where did you find that?" The Thief leaned out and took it from him. It clinked against exposed bone. "I haven't seen one in such a long time. I'd forgotten what they looked like. I thought the Spectress had destroyed them all." She handed it back to Prewitt and cleared her throat.

"It was after Seraphina's twelfth birthday that everything changed. She became a different girl. For a long while, she wept whenever she played with her music box, and then she stopped playing with it altogether. She gave up on living. Every time I visited, she begged me to bring her poison to drink.

"I knew I had to do something. I had to find a way to help her escape, but the trouble was that I didn't know where we could go. I spent all my time in the mountain library, and finally, I read of a place across the desert, in the unknown lands beyond our kingdom, where people like my sister are not feared just because they were born different. However, when I told Seraphina about it, she refused to leave.

"I knew I had to find a way to give her hope. I plotted and

planned, and I pressed the mountain sages for information, knowing they held all the secrets of the past. They told me about the Firebird Feather. It was the most sacred object in all of Lyrica, but after a thousand years, it had been forgotten, turned into nothing but a relic and a story. As Lyrica thrived and flourished in peace, the memories of darker times and the sacredness of their Feather were forgotten.

"The sages warned me that a Feather could only be given and that stealing one would be a terrible curse, but I didn't care. I would have happily taken any curse if it meant my sister might be happy."

Calliope's heart warmed. It was the kind of love her mother had shown her, the kind that sacrificed for someone else.

The Thief went on. "It was easier than I could have hoped. The sages had been right. Even the Queen didn't seem to care about the Feather any longer. It wasn't even guarded! I found it tucked back onto a shelf in the castle gallery, collecting dust. All I had to do was exchange it for a replica I had bought in the market, and I was out of the city before the *Queen's Barge* had even left the harbor.

"I gave it to Seraphina, and right away she seemed more hopeful. She told me that all she needed was a little more time with the Feather, and then she was certain she would be able to leave.

"I was overjoyed that we would soon begin our new life. But when I came to see her the next morning, she was not here. My sister was gone." She stopped talking.

"Gone? But I don't understand. The Wind said she's still here," said Calliope. "It said she's still a prisoner. We're here to save her."

The Thief looked at her, taken aback. "You really don't know, do you?"

Calliope glanced at Prewitt, but he looked as confused as she felt.

"The marked girl you're so determined to save is *the Spectress.*"

29

"You're lying." But Calliope saw the truth in the Thief's eye.

She felt her heart split in two, at sudden odds with itself. Ever since the Wind had told them about the girl, ever since she had felt the loneliness of her cries, Calliope had felt a kinship with her, but now . . .

It was awful, this feeling of being divided. How could she feel sorry for the monster who had murdered her mother? She wouldn't. She couldn't. She shoved away all the compassion she had felt. Anger. Anger was the way to deal with cruelty.

The Thief's voice scattered her thoughts. "That day, when I came and my sister was gone, I searched the mountains, frantic that something had happened. Finally I found her standing over the caldera.

"The Demon had felt her fear and sorrow and had

whispered to her heart in her solitude. It promised her power greater than she could ever imagine, had offered her vengeance against those who had hated her from birth, retribution against those who had locked her away and ignored her cries. It offered her freedom and power."

The Thief hung her head. "Why didn't I see? I should have known the Demon had found her. I knew the ancient story. We all did. But I was no better than the Firebird Queen. I'd forgotten the truth that stories can hold." The Thief swallowed and shook her head, the burned coils of her hair rustling.

"By the time I remembered, it was too late. My sister had taken the Feather to the Demon. I found her, holding it over the lava. I tried to stop her. I begged and screamed, but she couldn't hear me. I ran at her, tried to pull the Feather from her grasp, but—" The Thief broke off.

"What happened?" asked Calliope, her nails digging into her palms.

"I fell. My flesh melted away, and the Feather dissolved into fragments in front of my eyes. I saw the Firebird's magic leave them, and I heard the Demon rise up against its chains.

"Somehow, I managed to pull myself out of the lava, clutching the ruined fragments in my hands. I slipped from the mountains and crawled into the bog, where I lay in the coolness, surrounded by biting gnats. I wished for death, but it wouldn't come, and I knew. I had been cursed."

"That's horrible," said Calliope, and she loathed the

Spectress even more. Her sister had loved her, had sacrificed so much for her, and she had thrown it all away for selfishness.

"You must really hate her," breathed Prewitt.

The Thief shook her head. "She is my sister, whatever she has done, and I know she suffers. Suffering of the heart is far worse than suffering of the flesh."

Calliope couldn't speak. She didn't understand how the Thief could still feel compassion for someone who had caused her so much pain. Finally, she said, "Isn't there any way to break the curse?"

"Yes," said the Thief, and she reached into her cloak, pulling out the final token. "The Feather must be restored."

Wind, Woman, Thief. They had done it. They had found them all. Calliope stretched across and took the fragment from the Thief's palm.

For a moment, they both held their breaths, but nothing happened. The fragments did not glow. They did not re-form. They lay like three metal lumps.

The Thief dropped her face into her hands. "I will never be redeemed."

Calliope stared down at the tokens.

"Don't worry, Cal. We'll figure out the Song somehow," Prewitt said, trying to reassure her. He tugged down his jacket, and the metal piece in his pocket clacked against the conch shell.

Calliope looked up at the sound, a sudden thought thrilling through her. "Prewitt! Show me that silver piece again!"

Prewitt pulled it from his pocket, eyebrows knit.

Calliope lined up the three fragments in one palm and held the squished metal piece in the other. "What if the tokens aren't just pieces of a broken Feather? What if they're the Song, too?"

The Thief pulled her hands away from her face.

"Firebird feathers," whispered Prewitt. "You're right! You must be!"

Calliope ran to the corner where the heap of toys lay. Kneeling down, she began to dig through them. "We have to find the box! What does it look like?"

The Thief didn't answer, and Calliope turned around. "Don't you know where it is?"

"I'm sorry," said the Thief, and her voice held the weariness of years of suffering. "I do know where the box is, but knowing will not help you."

"Why not?"

"Because my sister took it with her."

For a long time, Prewitt and Calliope just stared at her, not wanting to believe it was true, but at last Calliope stood. "Then I'll have to go and get it."

"But, Cal, didn't you hear what she said? The Spectress has it."

Calliope turned to the Thief. "You must know some way we can get to it. Think."

The Thief looked up. "There is a secret way into the caldera. I can take you that far, but I can't help beyond that. If I get too close, the Demon will overtake me."

"It's all right. You don't have to get close. I can do it." Calliope turned to Prewitt. "You stay here, just in case something goes wrong."

"No way! I'm not letting you go by yourself."

Calliope opened her mouth to argue, but Prewitt cut her off. "I'm not staying behind," he said. "I'm not letting anyone else put themselves in danger while I stay safe. I'm the one who's going."

Calliope shook her head. "What if something happens to you?"

"If the Spectress kills me, the world won't end."

Calliope stamped her foot. "Well, I'm not going to let you put your life in danger for me, either!"

"I'm the other half of the moon!" Prewitt shouted back.

"So what? Is that all that matters to you? Your duty and being half of the moon?"

Prewitt stared at her. "Duty? That's not the reason at all."

"It isn't?"

Prewitt shook his head, and he realized that it was true. "When my father took you into the Cavern, it wasn't because of duty. It was because your mother was his friend." And saying it out loud, he realized that it was true. It hadn't been duty that had painted his father's face with sorrow. It had been the awareness that he was saying goodbye to his friend.

Prewitt stepped forward until he and Calliope were close. "I promised Granny Arila I would follow my destiny and come find you. For a long time, I thought that meant I had to keep you safe, but now I finally understand that my destiny isn't just about finding you. It's about friendship. Don't you see? You are my destiny, Cal. We're two halves of the moon. Please let me do this for you. Let me be your friend."

Calliope threw her arms around him, her heart smiling. They *were* friends after all. She had known it all along. "Promise you'll be careful, and if you aren't absolutely certain you'll be able to get away once you have the box—come back, and we'll think of something else."

On his way out the door, Prewitt paused. "You aren't going to do anything, right? You'll stay here until I get back?"

Calliope blinked, the picture of innocence. "Of course. What else would I do?"

Prewitt narrowed his eyes and held three fingers to his lips. "Waterman's Word?"

"Waterman's Word," said Calliope, and she was very glad that she was not a waterman.

The Thief led Prewitt through the mountains, and he couldn't help wondering if Calliope had agreed a bit too quickly.

He followed the Thief in and out of hidden crevices until they reached a particularly narrow fissure.

"This will lead you to the caldera," rasped the Thief. "Only a child can fit through. Firebird protect you, Bargeboy."

It was utterly dark inside the fissure, and the walls grew hotter as Prewitt slid farther and farther in, the reek of the

Thief's rotting skin replaced by the stink of sulfur. The narrow walls began to glow orange, and Prewitt knew that he was close.

Porous rock pressed against his ribs, and he held his breath, taking tiny steps closer and closer until at last, he saw the caldera.

The fissure opened at the very tip of a crescent-shaped obsidian floor that curved around the edge of the volcano. Across the floor, golden doors rose high and torches lined the rock on every side. Ash golems stood sentinel along the wall, their veins flashing, smoke rising up the walls of the towering chamber.

Not far from where Prewitt stood, the back of a golden throne flickered as if it, too, were made of liquid fire.

A moon-white hand grasped the arm of the throne, and fear tightened Prewitt's chest. The fingers were unnaturally long, lengthened by talon-like nails, dipped in gold.

Beside the throne was a delicate glass table, and on it sat a tiny wooden box.

He stifled a whoop. All he had to do was find a way to get to it without being seen. Even as he thought it, the hand plucked the box from the table, caressing it with delicate fingers before setting it down again.

Prewitt chewed his lip. He needed a distraction, something to—

The doors suddenly opened, heaved by two lines of marauders.

Cool air wafted around the caldera.

"Tell me you've found her!" a voice commanded from the throne.

Prewitt braced himself. The table wasn't too far, maybe twenty steps away. All he needed was the right moment. If he could snatch it and make it back to the fissure, he'd be safe.

"I-I'm sorry, Your Grace," stammered one of the marauders.

"I don't want your apologies. I want the girl!"

The marauder cringed. "She's here, Your Grace. The Falconer found her wandering the hallways."

Prewitt shook his head. They couldn't be talking about Cal. They had to be talking about someone else. Calliope was safe. She'd promised. She'd given him the Waterman's Word. His heart pricked. He'd given someone the Waterman's Word once, too.

A gentle laugh bubbled up the walls of the caldera. "It takes a lifetime to learn these mountains."

Prewitt shook his head, trying to rid himself of the dread hammering at his skull. He couldn't worry about Cal. He had to stay focused. This might be their only chance to get the box.

The Spectress stood, sweeping from the room, two men crawling on their hands and knees behind her.

Prewitt's gaze was locked on the box. He slipped from the fissure, reaching the table just as the Spectress disappeared through the doors.

He stretched out a hand and snatched the box from the table.

It was tiny, half the size of his palm and made of shining rosewood. He was about to turn and run back to the fissure when his eyes snagged on the lid.

What he saw turned his stomach to acid. It wasn't possible. What did it mean?

A hand grabbed his wrist, and Prewitt yelped, terror coursing through him as he bumped into the table, sending it crashing to the floor.

But his fear fell away when he realized who was staring down at him.

He let out his breath. "Dad!"

He wrapped his arms around his father, breathing in the scent of him. He still smelled like brine, even here, so far from the sea.

His father shoved him away. "What are you doing, boy? How dare you try to steal from the Spectress!"

The blood drained from Prewitt's face, and his energy trickled out onto the floor.

The eyes glaring down at him were not his father's at all. They were black and empty—just like a marauder's.

30

Ilsbeth wasn't the sort of girl who hesitated, yet here she was, hovering at the edge of the pond, unable to take another step.

"Ilsbeth? Are you coming?"

She looked up. The girls watched her, waiting for her to lead the way.

The Wild Woman stood in the pond, her hand outstretched. All around, the Glade was burning. The willows were flaming torches. There was no more time, and yet here she was, faltering. What was wrong with her?

"Girls," commanded Ardal. "We *must* go."

Ilsbeth took a step forward. She was about to wade into the water when she saw something shimmering among the reeds.

She bent down and picked it up. An eight-pointed star glimmered at her from the surface of a familiar button.

"We cannot wait!" said Ardal. "Our magic is nearly gone. The Wild Woman cannot hold the moon's light any longer."

Fi placed a hand on Ilsbeth's arm. "Do you want to stay?"

"I want . . ." Ilsbeth broke off. What did she want? She had told Prewitt and Calliope that she wanted to survive, but was that really true? Was that all she wanted? To survive in someone else's past?

She looked at the girls gathered around her, their eyes flickering in the firelight.

"I want to fight," she said, wrapping her fist around the button, and when she turned away from the pond, the Glade Girls followed.

31

Of course, Calliope never had any intention of staying behind while Prewitt put his life in danger. If their friendship was his destiny, then it was hers, too. They were a team, two halves of the moon, and she was going to do her part to give him the best chance possible.

Her plan was to create a diversion. She would walk straight to the caldera doors and knock. All eyes would be on her as Prewitt went for the box. It would be dangerous, but she only needed to buy them enough time to get the box and play the Song.

But things had not worked out the way she'd planned.

First, she'd gotten lost.

Then, the Falconer had found her.

Or rather, one of his birds had. It flew low around the corner, shrieking at the sight of her, and Smith had come running.

He had dragged her through the passages, his birds flying ahead of him.

His face was ashen, and he kept muttering to himself. "She'll have to give her back now. She'll have to; she'll have to."

The sound of rushing water rose to meet them as they came to the edge of the river, cutting its way through the heart of the mountain. It raged harder than ever, sending swirls of mist twisting through the air.

"Tell the Spectress that the Falconer has brought her the Lost Princess of Lyrica," Smith shouted over the roar of the water. The marauders lowered a heavy drawbridge.

On the other side, immense golden doors undulated in the misty torchlight. A dozen marauders stood to each side of the doors, faces grim. At the sight of Calliope, they moved into formation, every man pushing with all his might, and the doors swung slowly inward.

A great blast of searing heat sent Calliope's hair billowing. Her curls crackled, and the river mist evaporated, and for a moment, she caught a glimpse of molten rock boiling in the caldera on the other side of the doors. She covered her face, the stench of sulfur burning her eyes, and when she peeked between her fingers, the Spectress appeared.

A white veil draped across her face, hanging down to her feet, and diamonds glittered like snowflakes across her white gown.

In the mist, she truly was a specter; even her movements credited her name as she glided toward Calliope, golden heels softly clicking on the pavers.

"At last!" she said, her words cool on the wave of heat.

Crawling behind her, heaving the jeweled train of her gown, were two men in blue jackets. They didn't look up, entirely focused on keeping the Spectress's train from scraping the golden floor.

Smith shoved Calliope forward. Ash golems roiled in the doorway, waiting for a command.

The Spectress's hand drifted upward like a floating feather. Her pale fingers trembled, golden nails flickering with the pulse of her golems' veins.

She peeled back her veil, as if removing an outer layer of skin, and for the first time, Calliope saw her.

Her skin was whiter than bleached bone, her facial features fragile, her cheekbones high and soft. She looked as if she had been carved from marble. There was no color in her at all. A cloud of gossamer hair hung down around narrow, dove-white shoulders.

Calliope shook her head, trying to match this beautiful woman with the image of a monster she'd created in her mind.

The Spectress stopped inches from Calliope, gazing into her eyes. Her pupils were on fire, halos of flame around black coal.

"So you are Lyrica's elusive *Lost Princess*." The Spectress's voice drifted like a lullaby, and she reached out a skeletal finger, tracing Calliope's cheek with a golden nail. "The last remaining Firebird Queen."

Calliope cringed backward as the needle-fine point

scratched her skin. She glared up at the Spectress. "I'm not afraid of you." She wondered if Prewitt had found the box yet, and she glanced back at the river. Could she escape that way? She could swim, but could she swim well enough to keep from being pulled under?

The Spectress fluttered translucent lashes. "You're either very brave or very naive." Her lips curved, and her head tilted heavily on her slender neck. "You've lived in a cave for your entire life," she said, sweeping her hand around, her nails sparkling with the glitter of gemstone stalactites. "This grandness must all be quite overwhelming."

"Not particularly," said Calliope. "It's still a cave, just bigger."

The Spectress's eyes blazed.

"What about my daughter?" interrupted the Falconer. "I was told that if I helped you get what you want, you would give me what I want."

The Spectress tilted her head, her eyes narrowed.

Realizing his error, the Falconer stammered, "I-I'm sorry, Your—Your Grace. I only meant to humbly ask if you might find it in your heart to—to—" He bowed, groveling.

"Oh my," said the Spectress with a trilling laugh. She closed her eyes and licked her lips. "Can you feel his fear, Princess?" She shivered. "It's intoxicating."

The Spectress beckoned to a nearby marauder, who ran across the drawbridge.

A minute passed, and they waited in silence.

The Spectress picked at her nails.

There was a crash from within the caldera, and the Spectress frowned, turning toward the doors.

But at that moment, the marauder returned, dragging a girl with him, and the Spectress turned back around.

The girl was slim, and there were dark circles beneath her eyes. Her ankles were shackled, and she trembled so hard that her teeth rattled.

"Look, child." The Spectress's voice oozed sweetness as she stepped toward the girl, floating a hand at the Falconer. "Your father has come for you."

Calliope saw hope sweep across the girl's face. She watched it brighten her eyes as the girl looked at the man who stood by the drawbridge.

"Go on," said the Spectress. "Go to him, and he will take you home."

Calliope couldn't breathe. Her heart hesitated, not trusting the moment.

The girl walked toward Smith on timid legs, and Calliope saw the Spectress's eyes glitter.

Smith fell to his knees, holding out his arms. "It's okay, my darling," he sobbed. "I've come for you." The birds bated on his shoulders.

The girl broke into a run. When she reached him, he recoiled, and she looked at him, confusion on her face.

"This is not my daughter," said Smith. He turned toward the Spectress. "My daughter's eyes were unusual. One brown and one gray."

Calliope stiffened. She knew a girl like that.

The Spectress shrugged. "Your daughter must have been one of the others. Who can remember? One girl is the same as any other. Take this one and go, while I am being merciful."

Smith's face was racked with pain. "What have you done with my girl? Tell me you didn't hurt her!" He reached out, pleading, but before he could come any closer, his body went rigid. He pressed his hands to his ears, veins pulsing at his temples.

"What are you doing to him?" asked Calliope. "Leave him alone!"

The Spectress laughed. "I'm not doing anything. It's the great Demon speaking to his heart."

Smith's shoulders were iron stiff as his pupils slid out of focus.

"Yes," whispered the Spectress. "Give in. There's no point in fighting."

The girl saw the change in the Falconer and turned to flee back across the drawbridge, but she wasn't fast enough.

The Falconer whistled, and his birds attacked. They pinned her to the ground, pecking at her cheeks. The girl screamed, covering her face.

"See how her hope betrayed her?" cooed the Spectress. "She believed her father really had come for her."

Calliope ran to the girl, waving her arms, trying to frighten the birds away, but the Falconer was there. He shoved her hard, knocking her back, and lifted the girl by the collar.

Before Calliope could do anything, the Falconer flung the girl into the river.

Her scream cut off as the rapids pulled her under.

Wind shrieked through the cavern, forcing the hot air up into a dense white cloud that hid the cavern ceiling.

The East Wind demands a drowning. Calliope sucked in a breath. "How could you?"

The Spectress shrugged. "*I* didn't do anything."

Her heels clicked as she sauntered toward the Falconer, and she reached out her fingers, caressing his cheek with her nails. "It's bliss, isn't it? Finally giving in and letting fear take over?"

She snapped her fingers, and he turned, marching into line with the other marauders, eyes black pools.

"It's so ironic." The Spectress turned back to Calliope. "The only ones not affected by the Demon's voice are children too weak to do anything to stop me."

She whirled and floated toward the doors.

"Come along, Princess! It's time to awaken a new age. *The Age of Fear.*"

32

It was one of the men in blue jackets who dragged Calliope through the golden doors and into the caldera, his puff of white hair static in the dry heat.

They nearly ran into the Spectress, the jewels on her train cutting Calliope's feet, when she came to a sudden halt.

"What's this?" the Spectress sneered. "A *boy* in my caldera?"

Calliope's heart was a stone, sinking into mud. *Please don't let it be Prewitt*, she begged. *Please don't let it be Prewitt.*

But it was.

Worse than that, the one who held him, who pulled his arms back so harshly that it looked like they might break, was Meredith.

"No," whispered Calliope, seeing Meredith's blank eyes.

The Spectress looked over her shoulder, showing her teeth.

"I think you'll find the Bargemaster is not as amenable to helping you as he's been in the past."

She clicked forward, pressing a nail beneath Prewitt's chin, forcing him to look into her eyes.

"Isn't this sweet? The Bargemaster's brat come to the rescue. How did you get in here, little one?"

Calliope tried to step forward, but the man held her tight.

Prewitt glared up at the Spectress. "If you don't let the Princess go, you're going to regret it."

The Spectress blinked, and then she laughed, her hand dropping down to her belly. "Isn't that just like a child? Your own father holds you captive, will *kill you* if I whisper the word, and yet you still have hope that everything is going to work out."

She turned to Calliope. "What about you? Are you still so naive?"

Calliope glared up at her. "Nothing you can do will make me give up hope."

The Spectress's lips curved into a sneer, and Calliope knew at once that she'd said the wrong thing. She should have pretended to despair, should have begged for mercy, but it was too late. Before she could say anything more, the Spectress lifted her fingers to her lips and blew on her golden nails.

They erupted into flames.

"Prewitt!" shrieked Calliope.

The fireball struck him square in the chest, and he crumpled to the floor at the Bargemaster's feet.

Calliope screamed, wrenching against the calloused hands that held her, but she couldn't escape. She kicked and tugged until her energy was gone.

"Let her go," said the Spectress sweetly. "Let her come and see what her hope has done." The hands gripping Calliope's arms instantly released.

She tripped forward, falling down at Prewitt's side.

His face was deathly pale, and the wound in his chest smoked.

Her tears splattered his freckles and tumbled down his caramel cheeks. He had come for her, had sacrificed himself for her. Not for duty or for the world but because they were friends.

"Now do you see? Hope will not save you. Not here. Your only hope lies far behind you. You should have listened to your elders, should have understood that your only chance at perfect hope was in that cave. But the moment you stepped across the threshold, you entered *my world*, and this world has no room for hope. The Demon and I have made sure of that."

Calliope reached for Prewitt's hand. "Prewitt?" she called, his name lodging in her throat. Since he had come into her life, she hadn't been lonely, but now, the only real friend she'd ever had—the only one not made of paper—was gone.

Another death was all her fault. The Wild Woman's words came back to her. *Do not answer with sorrow! Answer with rage!*

Calliope felt the heat rushing into her, coursing through her veins. This was no time for sorrow. This was a time for anger.

Calliope pressed Prewitt's hand to her cheek. "I'm going to make this right," she whispered, and as she said it, a tiny wooden box slipped from his fingers and onto the glass floor.

Calliope sucked in a breath. Prewitt had done it! He had found the box! She reached out, picking it up.

"That's mine!" hissed the Spectress. "Give it back."

Calliope ignored her. She opened the lid. Inside, a spindle floated in purple velvet.

She yanked the fragments from her fingers, sliding them into place on the spindle.

"What are you doing? Stop it!"

The fragments glowed and became one. "It's going to be okay, Prewitt," she said, and she knew in her heart that it would be. The Firebird would come. It would destroy the Spectress and punish her for everything she had done. The joy of that thought, the anticipation of it, filled Calliope's heart.

She grasped the crank between her fingers and wound and wound until it couldn't be wound any more, and then she let go.

The Song was tinny, barely audible above the bubbling lava and the Spectress's ragged breaths.

Calliope looked up. At any moment, the Firebird would appear from the sky. It would dive in and avenge them. She held her breath, waiting.

The Song slowed and died.

But the Firebird did not come.

33

"Did you really think that my music *box* would call the Firebird back?"

Calliope's gaze plummeted from the sky. She didn't understand. Why hadn't it worked?

The Spectress's eyes blazed. "The Firebird Queen," she scoffed. "The perfect, hopeful child who saved Lyrica from darkness and brought the Firebird winging to her side."

The volcano shuddered, and the glass cracked beneath their feet.

"Oh, I loved that fairy tale more than anyone once. What better hope can there be for a girl locked away in the dark than the fantasy that she, too, might sing a Song so hopeful that the Firebird would come to her rescue?"

The Spectress clutched at her skirts. "I counted down the days until I turned twelve, and when that day finally came, I sang. I sang with all the belief in Lyrica. I put my hope in the Firebird, and I knew it would come and rescue me. I believed as you believed a moment ago." Her eyes blazed and her fingers trembled. "But it was all for nothing. Don't you see? Don't you understand yet?" Her pupils were infernos. "The Firebird does not care about suffering, or children, or cries of loneliness in the night. It has abandoned us all."

She grabbed a handful of Calliope's curls, yanking her head back. "There is only one way forward for Lyrica now. You must embrace fear, must accept the freedom that comes with the Demon's power."

Calliope's eyes brimmed. "The Firebird *will* come," she said. "I know it."

The Spectress glared down at her. Then she screamed, "Bring me my dagger!"

It was the Bargemaster who brought it.

The Spectress's breath was ragged and sweet as she pressed the obsidian blade against Calliope's throat. "It is time for this tale to die. This wretched story of hope will end with you, and no other child will ever have to believe it again."

Calliope looked up at the opening of the caldera, her confusion a deepening chasm within her. What had she done wrong? Why hadn't the Firebird returned?

The dagger broke her skin, and a droplet of blood dribbled onto her collarbone. But before the blade could go any deeper, a sound permeated the volcano. It bounced off the chamber walls and echoed all around.

The Spectress tilted her head, and the dagger hesitated at Calliope's throat.

Somewhere, a bell was tolling.

It rang and rang, and as the sound grew louder, a light shimmered on the surface of the lake.

Calliope squinted, trying to make it out.

And then she saw it!

The Firebird's head. Its glittering ruby eyes!

The Spectress sucked in her breath. "It can't be!"

And she was right. It wasn't.

It was the golden figurehead from the *Queen's Barge*, floating in the middle of the lake, and standing atop it were the Glade Girls.

For a moment, Calliope didn't understand, but then she realized what must have happened. They had rung the fog bell, and the patron star had brought all that was left of the Barge back to the place where it had been forged.

The girls waited like a held breath, whips at the ready, moonflowers glistening in their hair. Their skirts floated in the heat, twisting around their ankles like petals in a breeze. All at once, they shrieked and leaped onto the crescent floor, fearless and shining.

Behind them, the figurehead sank, ruby eyes winking as it slid beneath the surface.

A *crack* sent the Spectress reeling backward, and her dagger clattered to the glass floor. Her marble fingers grasped at the wet green plait that bit into her narrow throat.

"Are you all right?" Ilsbeth asked Calliope, her muscles taut as the Spectress struggled against her, eyes bulging.

Calliope nodded. "I can't believe you came," she said.

"You were right. We are not just girls," said Ilsbeth, her eyes flashing. "We are sisters, and sisters don't let each other fight alone."

Around the caldera, the girls spun and cracked their whips, attacking without hesitation, but Hazel cried out from across the cavern, and Ilsbeth's eyes flicked around, assessing.

"The ash golems are too strong here," she said, and Calliope saw it was true.

Although the girls' whips were lobbing off arms and heads, they whirled instantly back, and leafy pouches struck only to evaporate in the heat.

Ilsbeth turned to Calliope, tightening the whip around the Spectress's throat. "You have to put an end to this."

"How? I tried to call the Firebird, but it didn't work."

Ilsbeth nodded down at the dagger on the floor.

Calliope shook her head, taking a step back. "I can't!"

"You have to! It is the only way."

"There *has* to be another way, Ilsbeth. I'm not a murderer."

"I led the Glade Girls here because of you. If you let them die, you will be murdering them."

Calliope felt panic well within her. The Song had failed. What other choice did she have? Maybe Ilsbeth was right; maybe this was the answer. How many lives could be saved with just this one death?

Looking around, she saw that the Glade Girls were nearing exhaustion.

She swallowed and, bending down, she traded the rosewood box for the blade. It was like ice in her hand.

The Spectress glared at Calliope, and her pupils suddenly erupted as her lips parted. "Demon, arise." The words squeezed from the Spectress's constricted throat, but they were enough.

"What is happening?" Ilsbeth's hand flinched as the white of the Spectress's eyes burned until the sockets were nothing but flames.

The mountain shuddered, the magma frothed, and the Demon rose.

It shook lava from curving black horns, and the din of its rattling shackles wrested boulders from the walls. They crashed down into the lava.

"You have to do it!" shouted Ilsbeth, flinching as magma sizzled against her cheeks. "Do it now!"

Fi screamed, and Calliope saw her fall to the floor, her dress aflame.

Calliope made her decision. The Firebird hadn't come, but justice still had to be delivered. Evil could not be tolerated. "You killed my mother. You killed my friend. You have tormented my kingdom for twelve years." The dagger floated high on the wave of her anger, but before it could crash down, someone shouted.

"Cal, wait!" Across the caldera, Prewitt lifted himself to his elbows, coughing.

Calliope gasped. "Prewitt! You're okay!" She couldn't believe it.

He pushed himself to his feet, staggering toward her, his red jacket in tatters.

"Stay there!" she screamed, but Prewitt ignored her.

He sprinted forward, dodging globules of magma and chunks of falling rock. His chest heaved as he took in gasps of sizzling air that was getting harder and harder to breathe.

His eyes were frantic. "Where is the box?"

Calliope shook her head, glancing toward the floor where it lay. "The Song didn't work, Prewitt. I tried, but I did something wrong."

Prewitt bent, picking it up. "No you didn't. It was me."

"What do you mean?"

He held out the box. "Look at the lid, Cal."

She did, and for a moment, she didn't understand what she was seeing. There, set into the wood, was the symbol that had appeared on the deck when they had first run from the golems. *Two halves of the moon.*

"I don't understand," she whispered.

Tears spilled down Prewitt's cheeks. "It's not me. I'm not the other half of the moon. I was wrong. Don't you see? It's her."

Calliope shook her head. "It can't be. It doesn't make any sense." She gazed into the Spectress's flaming eyes.

Two sides

Once divided

Moon's halves must be united

"If you kill her, you'll lose," said Prewitt. "We all will. The Demon will win."

"But the Barge—the symbol on the deck."

Prewitt thought back, trying to remember exactly how it had appeared. "I thought it was because I was there, but it must have happened when the ash golems' fire hit the deck. The Barge knew the Spectress's magic."

Calliope shook her head. She didn't want to believe it, didn't want it to be true. Ever since she had learned that the marked girl was the Spectress, she had refused to think about how similar their stories really were. They had both been kept in the dark. They had both been painfully lonely. And they were both angry.

But that was where the difference really lay. Because if the Wild Woman had taught her anything, it was that anger could be fed by either hope or fear, and she and the Spectress had chosen different paths.

"What are you waiting for?" screamed Ilsbeth.

Calliope and Prewitt locked gazes, and he nodded. "You can do this," he said. "You're the daughter of the Firebird Queen."

Calliope swallowed. She knew what she had to do, but knowing didn't make it easier.

Prewitt waited alone as she stepped forward without him.

"Let her go," Calliope called to Ilsbeth.

Ilsbeth's jaw tightened. "But she's evil. She killed your

mother! She killed my parents. If you let her go, she'll kill us all."

"I know, Ilsbeth. But this is not the way. Take the Glade Girls and run." She pointed at the crevice that Prewitt had snuck in through.

Ilsbeth's cheeks flushed. "Run? We came back to help you! Now you're sending us away?"

The lash dropped from the Spectress's neck, and Ilsbeth stepped back, shoulders tense and hands trembling, but she did not leave.

Calliope stepped in front of the Spectress.

"Seraphina!" she shouted.

It was a name the Spectress had forgotten, and when Calliope spoke it, the Spectress's eyes flickered, and for the briefest moment, the fire within dampened.

The Wind had said that the girl was still a prisoner in the mountains, and Calliope could see the truth of it in the Spectress's flaming eyes. The Demon was her master.

Calliope took a deep breath; then she ran forward, flinging her arms around the Spectress's waist and pressing her cheek against the beaded bodice.

"I forgive you, Seraphina," she whispered, and with those words, something dark released its teeth from her heart and flapped out of the caldera. "I forgive you for what you did when you gave up hope and gave in to fear. I'm so sorry that the Firebird didn't come when you needed it, but it isn't too late. Hope is still the strongest magic of all. It can still set you free."

The Spectress blinked rapidly, and her pupils shifted from red to silver.

The Demon screamed, rising up, squeezing its bellows so that a deadly tide of magma swept around the caldera.

"We can call the Firebird," said Calliope. "We can do it together." She pressed the box into the Spectress's hands.

"I don't know how to be hopeful anymore," said the Spectress, and her voice was small—a child's voice.

"Then I'll be hopeful for both of us," said Calliope.

They held the box between them, and Calliope turned the crank once more. The golden cylinder spun, and this time everything ceased. The lava did not bubble, the wind did not blow, and the falling boulders hung, suspended above their heads.

Everything was absolutely still as the Song played.

When it had finished, the box vanished, and in its place was the flaming golden Feather, whole and restored.

There was a great flash of light, and the caldera erupted with song as the Firebird appeared from a blazing tatter in the sky.

This was not a song that could be held within any box. It was pure hope folded into an uncontainable melody.

The Firebird soared into the volcano, its brilliant feathers an eruption of warmth and light that radiated across their upturned faces and sparkled in their eyes. The Firebird had returned at last! The wonder of it danced in their hearts as the Firebird glided, triumphant, into the caldera, its Song melting into every stone, mending cracks and crevices. The melody drifted down the Firebird's wings and seeped into their hearts, and the broken places there began to mend, too.

They watched as the Firebird's fiery eyes flashed and it tucked its wings close, diving toward the Demon with outstretched talons.

The Demon howled, batting at it, bellows constantly pumping, but the Firebird did not falter. It tilted its wings, riding the current of its Song as it glided around the Demon's horns, blazing chains streaming from fiery tail feathers.

Round and round the chains wrapped, weighing the Demon down, pulling it beneath the molten surface until, with a final, infernal howl of fury, it sank back into the recesses of the world, and the surface of the lake hardened into shining black stone.

The Firebird circled one last time.

Calliope and Prewitt and all the Glade Girls watched the Firebird rise up into the sky. For a moment, it hung above the caldera, flaming wings spanning the opening.

How strange, thought Calliope, for it suddenly occurred to her that fire itself had been the source of both their fear and their hope.

After the Firebird had gone, they turned to the Spectress.

Her white gown fell in limp folds around her, and her hair hung in curtains across her small, pale face.

Calliope and Prewitt sucked in their breaths.

The Spectress was a child once more. It was unnerving to

see her this way, fragile and small, and it was impossible to imagine how anyone could be afraid of her. Yes, she was different, but neither Calliope nor Prewitt could see why that should cause anyone fear. If the mountain people had shown this child love and compassion, then she might not ever have joined with the Demon at all, and the prophecy might not have come to pass. It was a sobering thought.

Meredith ran toward them. He gathered Prewitt and Calliope into his arms. "Thank the Emperor you're all right."

Cedric and Old Harry joined them, glaring down at the fragile figure sitting in a heap on the floor. There were holes in their pants, and their knees were burned from crawling after the Spectress's train.

"Don't be fooled," said Cedric. "She may look like a child, but this is still the woman who tormented us."

Calliope shook her head. "The evil heart of the Spectress is gone, trapped with the Demon beneath the earth."

"How do you know that for sure?" said Ilsbeth. "How do you know she won't grow up and become the Spectress all over again?"

Calliope tilted her head, thinking; then she knelt, holding out the Firebird Feather.

The child blinked up at her.

"I cannot let you stay in Lyrica, Seraphina," she said gently. "It wouldn't be safe for you. You wouldn't be happy. But I want you to take this Feather and begin a new life someplace else."

The child sniffled. "I'm all alone, just like before."

"You are not alone, sister."

The Thief stepped into view. A fresh layer of skin had grown across her bones, and as she walked toward them, they saw hair sprouting in whorls from her head, flowing down in tight, shining curls.

The child who had been the Spectress pressed the back of her hand against her mouth. "Nuria?" she asked. "Is that you? I thought I'd lost you forever."

The Thief reached out and pressed a hand to the child's cheek. "Didn't I promise that I would take you to find the unknown cities across the desert? Come, let us go and begin a new story, one where we can finally be happy."

The child wept, and the sisters embraced.

Above the caldera, the sky shifted into blue, and for the first time in many years, the warm rays of the dawning sun smiled down onto the peaceful heart of the mountain.

EPILOGUE

The final strains of the Firebird Song rang across the kingdom, and when the people of Lyrica awoke, they found the world utterly changed. The rain had dried up, and the sun rose, warm and benevolent, in the cloudless sky. Their gardens, which had been mud-choked for more than a decade, sprouted overnight, and the promise of new life materialized in bright spring blossoms.

The mountain was reborn. The hallways were blanketed with fresh growth, and vibrant flowers grew on hillocks that served as graves for the many who had died there.

The marauders returned to themselves, slaves to their fear no longer. But shame filled the space where fear had been, and most could not bear to return to their families. Instead, they struck out across the desert in the company of a small white-haired girl and a tall woman covered in scars. None of them knew what they would find beyond the sea of sand, nor how long it would take them to reach the cities beyond, but they pressed on, buoyed by the hope of a fresh start.

Calliope had been sorry to see that the Thief still carried the marks of her curse into her new life, but then she supposed they were all a bit scarred. They had survived a terrible thing, and the wounds and bruises, painfully earned, would remind them of their ability to overcome and to rise above whatever trials these new days might bring.

When the Falconer left the mountain and saw Ilsbeth, standing with the other Glade Girls, he had cried out. He knew her at once as the daughter he had lost. They spent a long time talking, trying to understand how they had been separated, and although they were both cautious, they were open to the possibility that they might be happy now that they had found each other.

The other girl, the one who the Spectress had tried to pass off as Smith's daughter, sat healthy and unharmed, humming beside the bog, which was now a daisy-dotted meadow. She chattered to anyone who would listen about the girls and the boy who had saved her when they hauled her into a longboat that just happened to be going downriver.

Prewitt and Calliope could hardly believe it when they stepped out into the sunshine and saw Jack waving wildly at them from the quarterdeck of the *Queen's Barge*. She was moored at the edge of the river quay, bobbing gently in the fresh morning sunshine as if she'd been waiting all along.

"You can always expect mysterious things from the *Queen's Barge*," said the Bargemaster, coming up behind them. "She's no ordinary boat."

As soon as she boarded, Calliope ran down the steps to her bedroom and was surprised to find the three girls they'd rescued from the dungeons fast asleep in her bed, the thick comforter tucked up to their chins.

She looked around the room as their soft snores drifted to the painted ceiling.

Everything was exactly the way she'd left it, as if no time had passed at all. Her paper kingdom and all its creatures was restored. She had expected to feel at home, but instead, it felt strangely foreign, as if the journey had changed the room as much as it had changed her. It made her feel a little sad to think about how much she'd needed these animals before—this world. But now she had real friends, and she'd seen the real world, and it was time to leave this one behind.

She stood on the step, her hand on the doorknob, feeling the weight of the moment. It was time to move forward, to become someone new.

"Goodbye," she whispered, looking around the room one last time. "Thank you for being there when I needed you."

Her gaze caught on something clutched in one of the girls' hands. It was Brown Bear, and in the others girls' hands were Hippo and Lion. Calliope smiled and shut the door behind her.

The Bookkeeper sat in the carriage, surrounded by books. His fingers were bandaged, and when Calliope asked, he told her that while he had been under the Demon's enchantment, the Spectress had forced him to write new histories. He had scribbled thousands and thousands of pages in a trance, had written until his fingers bled, and then he had written some more.

"You are very like your mother," he said, peering down his glasses at her.

"Did you know her well?" asked Calliope.

"Quite well," he said. He tilted his head. "I wonder what you will become now that the Song is in the air."

"What do you mean?"

The Bookkeeper rubbed a hand over his scalp. "Nothing, nothing. Just an old man's ramblings." Calliope left him staring out the window, deep in thought.

They all helped prepare the Barge for the return to the castle.

Prewitt and Jack scurried around the deck, following the Bargemaster's commands with feverish enthusiasm, and they were ready to leave before midday.

Although it had never been done before, necessity placed the Glade Girls at the oars, and Old Harry patiently guided them through everything they would need to know to keep the Barge on course.

"The river will do most of the work," he said. "We'll just use the oars to guide her home."

Prewitt went to join his father on the poop deck. The Bargemaster cleared his throat. "When we get home, there will be much to rebuild. The Princess will need support as the king-dom adjusts and as life returns to some kind of new normal."

Prewitt nodded. "I know," he said.

Meredith rubbed at his mustache. "I thought I was doing the right thing, keeping Calliope in that Cavern. But now I think she would have found hope no matter where she was. She's an extraordinary person. I should have seen it before. I should have seen a lot of things before."

He cleared his throat. "I owe you an apology, Prewitt. I shouldn't have kept so many secrets, but I was afraid of what would happen if you knew the truth." He took off his cap. "Will you forgive me?"

Prewitt swallowed, nodding. "I'm sorry, too, Dad. I'm sorry I broke my oath, and I'm sorry I didn't understand how much you had sacrificed for—"

Meredith pulled him close, cutting off the words.

After a moment, they separated, closer than ever before.

Meredith held out his cap. "What do you think?" he asked. "Are you ready to begin your apprenticeship?"

Prewitt gasped. "Really?"

Meredith nodded. "You've earned it, and you are twelve, after all."

Prewitt whooped, grabbing the cap and tugging it down onto his head. "Cal!" he shouted. "Look!"

She was standing on the figurehead, and she wobbled when she turned, but she grinned.

Prewitt felt Ilsbeth watching him, and he flushed.

She stared intently at him, the oar handle in her lap.

Prewitt went to her, and he stood for a second, not sure what to say.

Ilsbeth thrust out her fist, and Prewitt flinched, shutting his eyes.

"I am not going to strike you," said Ilsbeth, taken aback.

Prewitt opened one eye, and Ilsbeth opened her hand. There in her palm was Prewitt's missing button. He took it, and they both spoke at once.

"Thank you for—"

"The Princess said—"

Ilsbeth pressed her lips together, and Prewitt laughed.

"You first," he said.

"The Princess told me what you did. She told me that you went into the caldera all alone."

Prewitt rubbed the back of his neck. "I got caught."

"That doesn't matter," said Ilsbeth. "You were brave. The Princess couldn't have succeeded without you."

Prewitt scratched his nose. "You were the brave one. You were the one who *really* saved us. You and the other Glade Girls."

Ilsbeth crossed her arms. "We are *both* brave."

"All right," said Prewitt, grinning.

"Prewitt!" called the Bargemaster. "It's time!"

Prewitt ran to join his father at the tiller. The Bargemaster's face was relaxed. The pallor that had been a constant part of him was gone, and his skin was already darkening beneath the new spring sun.

He looked down at Prewitt. "Remember what to do?"

Prewitt nodded.

"Go on, then."

He stood tall. "Oars across, and sit ready!" he bellowed, just as his father had instructed.

Cedric demonstrated, and Jack and the Glade Girls copied him precisely while Old Harry called encouragement from where he lounged on the steps of the quarterdeck.

Meredith patted Prewitt on the back and tilted his chin toward the prow. "Go on, now, make sure the Princess doesn't fall off, will you?"

Calliope was lost in her thoughts, twirling the golden Feather between her palms as she stared out ahead of them. The Thief and the Spectress had insisted that she keep it, neither one feeling that it would be right to take it with them. But she wondered what the Feather really meant now. Was it still a source of power that bonded spirits and humans? Or had it changed with everything else?

She supposed that the answer didn't matter. The Feather's value was in more than magic. It held the memory of everything they had suffered and accomplished, and it was a symbol of a hope that could never truly be extinguished. She knew that she would do whatever it took to protect that memory.

Prewitt moved forward, letting his father's voice pour over him as it rang across the deck. "Right, now. Easy, all."

The oars came up out of the water, and the Barge drifted downriver, smooth and free in the sunshine.

New life teemed along the riverbank. They passed a crane,

gently dipping its beak into the water. A family of ducklings bobbed with the current. Lilies, primroses, and bright pink monkey flowers bowed as the Barge floated past.

"It doesn't even feel like the same world," said Calliope as Prewitt climbed up next to her.

"I'm not sure it is," he said. "The Song will be in the air for a while. There's no telling what it will do."

"What does that mean?" asked Calliope. "The Bookkeeper said something similar."

The corner of Prewitt's mouth quirked. "I have no idea," he admitted. "It's just something I've overheard the men saying."

They sat together, shoulder to shoulder, and Calliope said, "I'm sorry you weren't the other half of the moon."

"It's all right," said Prewitt, and he was surprised to find that he meant it.

At first, it had been excruciating to realize that he'd gotten it wrong. Granny Arila and the Bookkeeper had been so confident. When he realized that the prophecy didn't mean him, it had been hard, but he'd known that he still had a duty to do whatever he could to help. He hadn't run away—even though he'd been scared.

"Maybe I'm not the other half of the moon," he said, "but believing I was gave me the courage to come and find you. It helped me become someone different, someone brave. Besides, I don't need to be the other half of the moon anymore. Finding you, helping call the Firebird back, that's enough. I'll never regret being a part of this."

Calliope smiled and squeezed his hand. "Neither will I," she said.

As they rounded the final bend toward home, they saw the turrets of the castle rising on the cliffs, shining pink in the light of the setting sun.

"Listen," said Calliope. "Do you hear that?"

Prewitt's eyes pricked. A thousand voices were raised in harmony, floating out across the lapping sea. They sang a song that Prewitt had heard before, and he listened as the Barge drifted into the harbor, the figurehead glowing as if lit from within.

Calliope stood, lifting the Feather high, as the song rose to meet her.

> *It will return on wings of flame*
> *And our tears will be no more*
> *When at last our Queen comes home*
> *And the Firebird rides to shore.*

Prewitt's heart swelled, his emotions overwhelming him.

He had started this journey to avenge Granny Arila's death, but it had become so much more than that.

He'd learned what it meant to be a friend, how to follow instead of lead, and most important of all, he'd discovered that being the Bargeboy wasn't about the *Queen's Barge* at all. It wasn't about duty or sacrifice—not really.

It was about friendship. It was about this strange, brave girl standing beside him.

She had shown Prewitt what hope really meant.

She had shown them all.

The Barge pressed against the sand, and the crowd wept as Calliope stood, the Firebird Feather blazing in her hand and ashes in her curls.

She truly was the Firebird Queen, and she had come home at last.

ACKNOWLEDGMENTS

I began writing this story—or something vaguely like it—on the floor of a moldy laundry closet, surrounded by tacked-up pictures of firebirds, volcanos, rain puddles, and flaming feathers. At the time, my husband and I lived in a tiny apartment above a garage in the Seattle suburbs. It was autumn, and the rain smattering the roof was only interrupted by the grinding tremor of the garage door opening and closing. Mold climbed around the windows and spread across the ceiling, mist fogged the inside of the panes, and the carpet stank of mildew that left me clinging to my inhaler.

I could only *just* see the future I hoped for beyond the fog, but somehow, here I am, miraculously at the other side of a completed story. It is so fitting that I get to end this chapter by thanking all the people who supported and carried me when I certainly would have given up on my own.

Thank you to my sweet husband, Miah. "You can do absolutely anything you set your mind to," he said, and he never wavered from that statement, no matter the meltdowns, no matter the tears, no matter the incapacitating doubt. His love and sacrifice is the reason I was able to find space and time to create a new dream after many years of uncertainty and perceived failure.

Thank you to Heather Campbell, the best of cheerleaders and friends. When I sat on the beach in a downpour on my birthday and told her that I was giving up to languish in the mire of my own inadequacy, she scolded me. One five-minute call was all it took for her to remind me of what I truly wanted, and of how far I'd already come, and it galvanized me to give it one more try. Never underestimate the power of a friend who will tell you the truth whether you want to hear it or not. It is because of her friendship that this book exists. Because of her, I am a better person.

A huge thank-you to Pippin Properties, and especially to my agent, Sara Crowe, who read some of my earliest, messiest drafts and somehow saw potential. I couldn't have dreamed up a better agent, and I am amazed every day that she is somehow able to see my heart through all the rust.

When I first spoke to Mary Kate Castellani at Bloomsbury Publishing about this story, her enthusiasm was infectious. I am so grateful that she understood my characters, this world, and me. She knew what all of us needed, and because of her nudges and prods, I searched deeper, and this book became so much more than I ever could have expected.

Thank you to Allison Moore for stepping in as fabulous interim editor, and to everyone at Bloomsbury for everything they have done for this story and for me. A special hug to my creative team and to Vivienne To, who dressed up this book in such a beautiful way.

Thank you to my literary big sis and mentor, Martha Brockenbrough, who lets me bombard her with questions without ever making me feel small. Thank you to Sarah Hohner for taking the time to read and encourage me in spite of her very full life. Thank you to my Instagram book community who kept me company along this journey, and very especially to my friends Ruby Rumsey and Alena Bruzas. Thank you to Mom and Dad Flores who cried and prayed and walked with me through this process, and thank you also to my parents for keeping our home stuffed so full of books that the shelves collapsed.

And finally, thank you to my grandmother, a beloved first-grade teacher of many decades, who showed me the magical power of reading, the importance of teatime, and what unconditional love really meant. I miss you every moment.

S.D.G.

Visit Bloomsbury Online!

Find out more about our books and authors and download educator resources and catalogs on Bloomsbury.com. And connect with us on social media at:

/BloomsburyKids

/BookishBloomsbury

/BloomsburyYA